IN SEARCH OF NARRATIVE
IN AMERICA

UNFINISHED AND ABANDONED 1988-2001

⑤

THE COMPLETE WORKS OF CHRIS ERNEST HALL

CHRIS ERNEST HALL

In Search of Narrative In America

Unfinished and Abandoned
1988-2001

The Complete Works of Chris Ernest Hall

http://www.chrisernesthall.com

First edition

"Excerpt From a Conversation With a Madman" previously appeared in *Andy Warhol's Sister and Other Stories*, published 1990 and 1994.

ISBN: 978-0-9897943-5-0

Contents

In the spring of 1987, during my freshman year at UC Santa Cruz, R.E.M. released *Dead Letter Office*, an album of out-takes and b-sides from their first four albums on IRS Records. I lived in a dorm with many dedicated R.E.M. fans–it seemed like half my floor decamped one night to see them at the Oakland Arena when they played a make-up show for one that had been rained out at the Greek Theatre. I borrowed my neighbor's copy, curious to learn more about this group that seemed so highly regarded, both by rock critics and my peers, but sounded somewhat murky and low-key to my ears, which at that point were mainly listening to sonically punchy artists like Peter Gabriel, U2, and Talking Heads.

On first listen, the music didn't sound like much to me, just more of the same muffled vocals and chiming guitars. Only the songs "Ages of You" which I'd heard on the radio and "Toys In the Attic," which rocked, probably because it was an Aerosmith cover, made much of an impression on me. What I found more interesting than the music, though, were the liner notes that the group's guitarist, Peter Buck, had written; an entry for every song, sometimes an explanation of why the song didn't make it on an album, or just a small anecdote or piece of trivia.

Since that time, I've had a special place in my heart for those kinds of compilations, often referred to as "Odds & Sods" albums, after one of the first examples, The Who's 1975 collection of b-sides and rarities. Some of my favorite albums are of that variety–*Dead Letter Office*, Led Zeppelin's *Coda*, Smashing Pumpkins *Pisces Iscariot*, Pearl Jam's *Lost Dogs* (thought it suffers from being too long), and the aforementioned *Odds & Sods*. I've even made my own for bands like Soundgarden and U2 that haven't gotten around to doing it themselves.

But why should musicians have all the fun? When new editions of novels come out, all you get is a new introductory note from the author or a critical essay, if you're lucky. There seems to be a prejudice against opening up the kimono too far. I think that does them a disservice, though. For one thing, it reduces the opportunities for writers to fully exploit their back catalog. More importantly, though, it prevents younger and less experienced writers a valuable instructional opportunity.

As I pointed out earlier, listening to *Dead Letter Office* during my freshman year of college was part of the beginning of my critical sensibility; of no longer regarding the albums I loved as sacred objects delivered from on high by infallible, Olympian beings, but rather the product of actual people, thinking and making decisions. In his liner notes, Peter Buck suggests maybe they should have put "Windout" on *Reckoning*. He admits they got tired of a song–a comforting revelation; that even geniuses sometimes produce work that they themselves can get bored of, but that might still have value to others. He cheerfully admits that they should be sued for their cover of "King of the Road."

Realizations like that are huge breakthroughs for a young artist. ("They're human! Just like me!") They give you hope, and also inspire you to think seriously about how a particular piece of your work fits into the whole. You start to regard the immediate products of your inspiration as less sacred. You should feel free to reorganize and recombine piece of your writing at will, to create new stories and even books, no matter how much work it might be, if you realize that's what needs to be done.

It's also important to learn when to stop investing time and energy in a work. It's okay to walk away from something even if it's unfinished. There's an art to figuring out when you should stop working on a work; when you're blocked because you just need to figure something out, and when it's because you're finished but just don't know it. (More on that in the commentary to the story "One Setback After Another.")

Being an artist is just as much about the editorial function of deciding what to include, and what to leave out, as it is about the moment of pure, gushing creation. (Really, it's far more about the latter, but you must be careful not to scare the young artist too much.)

All of that is a long-winded explanation and justification for *In Search of Narrative In America*, which is my *Odds & Sods* or *Dead Letter Office*, or even, God forbid, *Pisces Iscariot*–a collection of my writing that was either never finished, abandoned because I got bored of it, or simply didn't fit into any of my other works or compilations.

As Peter Buck did in *Dead Letter Office*, I have included interstitial commentary, in italicized text, explaining the origin of each piece, context in my career, and the reason I didn't complete it, if there is one.

I have tried to avoid making substantial editorial changes to these pieces beyond cleaning up spelling errors, confusing formatting and unclear passages. However, in one case I couldn't leave well enough alone and found the inspiration to complete "Port Douglas." It is the concluding selection of this collection, for reasons that I hope will be obvious.

It seems fitting that I've chosen to begin this collection with a piece I wrote in fall 1988, right around the time I wrote "Television Set," the story that I usually use to demark the beginning of my adult, post-juvenilia career, and thus featured as the first selection in my collection Something Interesting to Read.

As with that short story, "The Death of Narrative" reflects a time when I was very influenced by meta-fiction such as the novels of David Lodge and Milan Kundera, and absurdist comedy in general, coming out of a period where I was collaborating on screenplays that were influenced by artsy, off-beat directors like David Lynch and Jonathan Demme.

This fragment is notable for being the first appearance of "Mike," an early alter ego of mine who later appeared in "Truth and Beauty", and finally evolved into the Michael of Notes For a Future Novel—*a young, earnest intellectual with no common sense or real-life experience, representing one part of the way I saw myself at the time.*

The Death of Narrative

The next morning, Mike woke up. He turned over, looked at the clock. It read ten minutes after nine. He realized that he had class in twenty minutes. His mind went over the intricate calculations. If he spent five minutes in the shower, got dressed in five minutes, and ran all the way to Porter, he would be on time to class.

Even in the miasma of awaking, Mike realized the impossibility of these calculations. He usually spent twenty minutes in the shower alone. There was no way he would be on time, so it was pointless to even go to class at all. Satisfied with this conclusion, he went back to sleep.

This time, he dreamed of trains. He was riding a long, thick pink train that was heading at great speeds across the countryside. He was the engineer, but the train needed no guidance, and indeed, seemed to be beyond his control.

Then, his responsibilities shifted. He was loading great quantities of coal into the engine of the train, but oddly, the coal was white instead of black. When he put the coal into the hatch, it did not burn, but merely sloshed around the engine like a great white sea of melted mashed potatoes. Then, he saw a tunnel. It lay like an unfathomable black hole in a high mountain-side. The tunnel lay in the center of a valley between two long ridges. The hole dilated and the train rushed in, heedless of the consequences.

There was a great concussion of noise and light. The last thing he remembered was drowning in gulfs of white liquid, and a memory of being an infant in a great vaulted cavern.

God, Freud would love me, thought Mike as he lay in bed. It was now ten thirty. He had to get up.

Ten minutes later, Mike was in the nearest practical equivalent to the white sea of his dream, a hot steaming shower. As he lathered his chest, he wondered what he was going to write about for his creative writing class. He reflected on his dream. Somehow it seemed too trivial to provide material for his story. He then considered writing a story which would deconstruct narrative. He would merely write a story describing a typical day of his with absolutely no conflict or plot whatsoever. It would demonstrate the futility of plot and since people tried to live their lives according to plot, it would show the futility of life.

Mike was so excited by this idea that he nearly forgot to wash his hair.

Later that day Mike began to write his story. It went like this:

The next morning, Mike woke up. As he lay awake in bed, he wondered just what Marie had meant when she had said "See you later" the previous day. Had she genuinely wanted to see him again, or was it just a social nicety? He attempted to resolve the question by remembered the exact tone of her voice, the expression on her face. Would he ever see her again?

With a groan, he realized that he had to get out of bed in order to be on time to his philosophy.

An hour later, freshly scrubbed and ready for anything, even something, he sat in a poorly lit classroom learning about the futility of narrative.

They were reading a text titled "The Death of Structure" by the French philosopher, Henri Lescaut. You couldn't really call it a book, since Lescaut believed that to publish anything, even non-fiction, was to succumb to the myth of narrative. Therefore the text was a loose assemblage of short passages arranged in no particular order, with no clear thesis. Although it was titled "The Death of Narrative," not all of the writing seemed related to that topic, and in fact much of it was description of various casual sexual encounters Lescaut had engaged in with his students.

All of which made it very difficult for the professor to figure out reading assignments. The professor, whose name was Richard Tablin, thought that Lescaut was ridiculous, and assigned him only to show how absurd the whole thing was. However, many of the students were very taken with his ideas, and had started to incorporate them into their papers, often by not doing them at all.

One of Lescaut's passages dealt with the "Death of Narrative" In it, Lescaut talked about coherence and how any attempt to structure experience basically rendered the experience meaningless.

The professor, who was entirely too clever for his own good, would lecture very sincerely on these topics, appearing to wholeheartedly agree with Lescaut while smirking all the while, making (he thought) it clear that the whole lecture was an exercise in applied irony.

Unfortunately, his students had been trained since infancy to suspend their critical faculties when listening to a teacher. So the irony was lost, and most of the students cheerfully accepted the death of narrative.

Especially Mike, who sat in the front row, trying to figure out how Lescaut's concepts applied to his creative writing class. If narrative was dead, what would writers substitute for it? Lescaut had stated in his book that writers had a duty to deconstruct the idea of narrative in their fiction and replace it with what he called the "representations of experience" in which the author would very carefully record his experiences, all the while avoiding any imposition of plot. In this way, the author would render himself unnecessary.

After class, Mike walked to class and very carefully avoided plot. Even ordinary conversation became difficult for him. He found that many people wished to engage in structure while they spoke. For example, Dave wanted to talk about what they were going to do this weekend.

Dave: So, why don't we go to the dance at Crown and the after-party at Crown-Merrill apartments?

Mike: But Dave, that sequence is totally arbitrary. why the dance, and then the after-party?

Dave: Well, dude, I mean, the dance is at nine, and the party won't be until midnight, probably.

Mike: But how do you know? It hasn't happened yet.

Dave: Uh, yeah, but I'm guessing that it will happen that way.

Mike: But don't you see? It's futile and random. The party could be after, or it could be before. It could not happen at all. All you're trying to do is impose your conception of structure on arbitrary events. It's pointless.

Dave: Dude, what's up? Have you like, taken some really bad acid?

After lunch, Mike had creative writing class. He, along with twenty other girls and boys, met twice a week to engage in narrative.

Mike wondered about relationships. If he went out with Marie, wouldn't that be succumbing to the chimera of plot? Relationships were the most tempting of narratives. You met, you fell in love, you went out together, you broke up, you ended up depressed. It was a clearly defined narrative path that mirrored the ritual of sex–foreplay, penetration, climax, afterglow. It was sex that worried Mike the most. Lescaut suggested in part of his book that relationships were the most futile of all of humanity's pursuit of narrative structure, citing that most literature revolved around "love stories." Lescaut maintained that only casual meaningless sex held validity.

A girl next to him was reading a story about a boy who found an old shoe one day, put it on, and discovered he could predict the future. It had a straightforward linear plot. When she had finished reading it, the workshop facilitator asked for comments.

Facilitator: Well, that was a very interesting story, Louise. Any comments?

Sheldon: Well I thought it was really neat, especially the part where he saw his future wife. I like the way you handled the images.

Mike: I had a problem with the plot.

Louise: You didn't like it?

Mike: No, it wasn't that. I just didn't like the fact that it had a plot. Narrative is dead, he announced to the class.

Andrew: Wait a minute. Narrative is dead? What are you talking about?

Mike: Well, according to Lescaut (he pronounced it carefully, like Less-Co) since the concept of author as authority had been deconstructed, the pursuit of plot is pointless. Only in the careful accumulation of "representations of experience" can there be any true meaning, in meaning is possible at all.

Mike's story was mostly based on reality. When he had finished it, he read it over carefully. He was pleased that he had managed to explain many of the concepts behind his story in the course of his day. There were no metaphors or images in his story, for Lescaut believed that all such things were inherently deceptive. It was pure reality, unflinchingly delivered, as refreshing as a cold shower after a hot day, compared to the artifice of the stories of the other students of his creative writing class.

Style bothered Mike also. If plot and narrative were dead, what about style? Lescaut referred to A. J. Ayer in his work, referring to Ayer's "sense-language" as a possible solution. Ayer considered normal speech deceptive and illusionary, since it relied on empirical constructs instead of precise description. Ayer thought that if language was replaced by a language that reported only what the senses saw, then confusion would be eliminated. Mike resolved to start writing only in "sense-language" to avoid untoward interpretation, for Lescaut taught that interpretation was the primal fallacy of the human brain. Interpretation came from people who couldn't deal with reality on its own terms.

Lescaut is a satire of French post-structuralism, though not a very deep one, possibly because I hadn't really studied it yet. My understanding was based mostly on reading about it in David Lodge's academic satire, Small World. *An early lesson for me that satire has to be based on deep knowledge and even love in order to be successful.*

When my mother read a draft of this introduction I left on her printer, she reminded me that I had been inspired to use that name by my sister's love for the Abbé Prevost novel Manon Lescaut, *which is something I had completely forgotten about. Since that is considered one of the first truly popular novels, it was an appropriate choice.*

"The Death of Narrative" is an example of one of the stories that I would get quickly lose interest in—not unsurprisingly, as any story whose subject is the futility of narrative is bound to have trouble getting anywhere. There's a germ of satiric possibility in the nihilist intellectual encountering the typically Hedonist UCSC student ("Dave") but in this story, it was handled too superficially to be more than a quick joke. I had better luck with it in Notes For a Future Novel, *probably because by that point I had actually studied enough literary theory to parody it effectively; instead of just getting my satire second-hand from David Lodge.*

There are fragments in this collection I believe I abandoned at the right time ("The Death of Narrative" being an example) but there are others where I wish I had kept writing. "The Mayor of Circumstance" is an example of the latter. I wrote this by hand on a bunch of yellow loose-lead notepaper in the summer of 1989 at Café Pergolesi in Santa Cruz. I had read The Crying of Lot 49 *the previous year in school—not for a class, but because someone I knew was, and I just borrowed it and read the whole thing in an afternoon.*

The Mayor of Circumstance

A few days later, when they were back in Santa Karla, Adrian attempted to explain what had happened while Michael had been away in the mountains.

Setting his empty cup down in the saucer and aligning it perfectly in the center, Adrian began.

"What you have to understand is, it was no big deal, really." He gestured obscurely with his fingers. Frequently when Michael listened to Adrian speak at length (he thought of it as speaking in paragraphs) he would examine his friend's hands. Adrian had a habit of discoursing on other's hand gestures as being important, and would frequently interpret at length. However, for one so attuned to the mannerisms of others, Adrian's hands had a dispiriting lack of coherency. They jerked and circled idly in no particular pattern, and certainly with no connection to what Adrian was saying.

Michael became so caught up in this observation that he missed what Adrian was saying next.

"–then she refused to see the obvious, naturally, that fax machines are an attempt by the Elite to make ordinary mail obsolete, thus rendering the W.A.S.T.E. system incompatible as an alternative to the federal mail monopoly."

As Adrian continued, Michael pieced together what he was saying with what Michael already knew about the topic under discussion.

Basically, Adrian had extrapolated his entire view of reality from the novel *The Crying of Lot 49* by Thomas Pynchon. Thus, he spent much time searching for clues of the operation of the Trystero. He had claimed to find evidence of that secret mail system operating in Santa Karla itself, on the boardwalk and even at the university, and offered to take Michael along to see that evidence.

Michael had refused, for the same reasons that he refused to go with his friends to go inside supposedly haunted houses. He thought that either resolution to the question–was it real or just paranoid delusions stemming from Adrian's extensive drug use in the 70s–was unsatisfactory. If it was delusion, Michael didn't want the sense of mystery destroyed.

And if there really was a super secret conspiracy operating in the world, Michael didn't want to know about it.

Michael, Adrian and a few others were loosely affiliated in a group which engaged in various "projects" which were, in the unkind words of Rachel, "intellectual joy-riding." This was an appropriate label, since frequently these projects involved co-opting an intellectual or metaphysical mindset and then recklessly applying said concepts to the world at large. They were all dedicated intellectuals, in a somewhat antiquated sense—for instead of safely pursuing abstractions in the state university which lay in the hills above the city, they instead attempted to force it on the public at large.

Postmodernism, structuralism, anarchism, and especially Situationalism all figured in their 'beliefs'—of course, one of their most cherished commandments was there were no beliefs. This profound contempt for structure of all kinds made most positive, constructive projects useless as a matter of definition. Unless of course, it was accompanied by a large dose of irony.

In moments of cynicism, which Michael had been susceptible to since a disillusioning experience with narrative when he had been an undergraduate at UCSK, he referred to their group in his own private mental language as a club—gathered together to pursue obscure intellectual games, much like others got together to play chess, or show slides or read poetry. Of course the middle-class, midwestern, and established bourgeois pretensions of the word club were the antithesis of everything Adrian and the others stood for, but the fact remained.

One night, Adrian had explained his parents' theories to the group at length, perhaps as an obscure form of apology for his own. Michael remembered some of the significant details.

Adrian had been raised by parents whose only pastime had been to watch network television every hour they could, searching for evidence that the International Communist conspiracy had infiltrated it. His parents' basic assumption was that communists sought to subvert industrial capitalism by channeling American ingenuity into increasingly unnecessary and useless products, such as eleven different brands of floor-wax, and umpteen varieties of sugary breakfast cereals, all made with the same recipe, but marketed separately.

"Of course, what Marxists say is that the production of increasingly unnecessary products is a hallmark of late-stage industrial capitalism, and my parents thought that the communists wanted to accelerate the process artificially by taking over the most prevalent source of advertisement in the United States–network television. Actually, my parents' theories made a lot of sense in a strange way–enough sense, at least, to get them kicked out of the John Birch Society."

Adrian went on to explain that Armand Hammer was at the center of the conspiracy, ideally situated with his close ties to the Soviet Union and ownership of a network of companies dedicated to proliferating as many consumer brands as possible.

I always liked the title the "Mayor of Circumstance" and kept it in an entry in my writing database where I kept random titles that I hoped to use someday in the future. It was most likely inspired by the XTC song "The Mayor of Simpleton" which was a hit in spring 1989. There is also a Grateful Dead song called "Saint of Circumstance" that might have somehow gotten into my brain subconsciously by looking at an album back cover, though it wasn't one I knew about while I was at Santa Cruz.

I finally got a chance to re-use it in Celebrated Summer, *when my fictional alter ego, Tim Page, uses it as the title of the story he writes about the homeless man his movie theater co-workers call the*

Mayor of Eden Street, who was in turn inspired by the character Spike Lee's movie Do the Right Thing.

The "Mayor of Circumstance" is perhaps most notable for being the first time that I used a fictional analogue for Santa Cruz, calling it Santa Karla. That was inspired by the setting for the 1987 vampire horror-comedy Lost Boys, *filmed in Santa Cruz, which was called Santa Carla, perhaps to avoid offending the locals who had so kindly hosted the movie production only to find it made prominent reference to the fact that for a while Santa Cruz was known as the murder capital of the United States. Changing it to a K is nonsensical, of course, since that letter isn't used in Spanish. It's either a brilliant meta-fictional move, or sheer incompetence. There is, after all, a very fine line between the two.*

Speaking of firsts, the following fragment, written sometime during my "first senior year," represents the first time I consciously based a character in my fiction on a friend of mine. "Susan" is based on the friend who would later inspire the character Helen Zachary in the Tim novels, though there isn't much in the story that would clue you into that, other than the description of her driving style. Is it creepy that I have one of my fictional analogues portrayed being in a relationship with another based on a female friend? Yes, yes it is.

Mike and Susan

Dogged. Mike mouthed the word silently to himself, feeling the way his tongue met and released the top of his mouth when he said it. Dogged. *Dogged.*

Exactly twenty-four hours previously his best friend in the world had used that word to describe him. Specifically, his attempts at romance.

Romance is a problematic word, almost as problematic as *dogged* since its adjective form, romantic, is also a genre of literature. It is important to point out that while this story might be *about* romance, it is not *a* romance.

Exactly twenty-four hours ago Mike had been romantically dogged. Mike was five-foot ten inches tall. Heterosexual. Blond hair, down to his neck in back.

Mike was one of the few people he knew who would let intellectual discourse get in the way of his relationships. Actually, to be honest, he had never really had a "relationship" in the sense that he used the word.

Relationship: Liaison between a girl and guy that involves sexual intimacy. Sex was the *sine qua non* of relationships. Without sex it was tangential, amorphous and insubstantial situation in which nothing was defined–a friendship. The only reliable yardstick for defining the way people related was the presence or non-presence of sex. This parallels biologists, who define all social interactions among animals as a function of mating.

Mike had a lot of problems with sex.

"I've become a celibate," he announced one night, apropos of nothing.

Susan kept driving, determined to keep on the right side of the road. At this point, a description of her driving might be a good metaphor for her character. When she was alone, she drove normally. Question: What do I mean by normally?

But when there was another person with her in the car, that caused Susan to sway from one side of the lane to the other, and to treat traffic laws as if they were inconveniences, optional suggestions for those who had the time and inclination.

"That's nice. By choice?" she said, turning and focusing her eyes on him.

"Well, not really. But that's beside the point. I've formulated an entire theory about human beings. All evil in the world comes from monogamous sexual relationships."

Of course all human thought is discourse in society. Celibacy is either insincere or an attempt at suicide. Mike knew this. Susan and Mike's relationship is deconstructive since any expression of desire would destroy it–but without that desire there wouldn't a relationship.

Perhaps it would help at this point if you stopped thinking of Mike as a character.

That last sentence always makes me laugh. There wasn't really anywhere I could with this piece from that point. The previous statement, though, is as good a description of the essential tension of the Santa Zita novels as any.

Now we come to the piece that gave me the title for this collection. I read Tristram Shandy *during winter quarter of 1990, so I'm guessing that's when I wrote this fragment. Once we again we see my alter ego Michael in action, this time taking a Kerouac-esque road trip–or trying to, at least. Once again my love of pastiche is evident, as I indulge myself in parodies of* Tristram Shandy *and* Virginia Woolf. *Plus a mention of my favorite baseball player of all time, Lance Blankenship!*

Narrative In America

At 10 am on June 21, Michael left the San Francisco Bay Area in search of narrative in America.

Once he passed the sign for Vallejo he shifted all the way over to the left, into the fastest lane, and settled his automobile in fifth gear and going at seventy miles per hour.

By 2 pm he had reached Route 49 in the Sierra foothills. Seventy-two hours earlier he had received a diploma in English Comparative literature from the University of Santa Karla after four years and two quarters of academic work.

When Michael saw the sign for Auburn he took the second exit, the one he remembered from ski trips with his parents–the exit leading to McDonalds, Burger King, Carls Jr.–all of which he passed on by.

He still had a quarter's tank of gas. His car was running as high as it ever did, sounding like it was just on the edge of going too fast, as if it were a horse in the home stretch.

Michael, when he was driving, sometimes thought of his car as a horse, for absolutely no reason, as he had never ridden a horse, or even been tempted to. Any animal larger than a cat frightened him. However, the spinning whine of the engine was horse-like.

"I've got a real knack for bad similes," he announced to himself as he looked for the sign for Route 49.

When he saw the sign for the highway, he spent a few minutes concentrating on getting on the highway. Once he was on 49 and could stop thinking entirely about driving, he narrated an imaginary Evening Magazine story about himself:

Route 49. Gold Rush country. One hundred and forty years ago, men came here to find nuggets of gold hidden in isolated streams, and jealously guarded the location of their stakes. Now, one man is coming back to the gold rush country in search of a different kind of nugget. The kernels of narrative hidden off the beaten track in the highways and byways of America–the stories and plots that make up life in America. In short, Michael Thomas is in search of... narrative in America.

Satisfied with this introduction, Michael started to imagine exactly how the spot would begin. First there would be a shot of his mid-80s Japanese sedan on sunlight-dappled roads surrounded by firs and redwoods. A curving road, of course.

Then, the show's personality, a blond woman in her 30s, who had been narrating the introduction while Michael was navigating the highways and byways, would actually be seen, standing outside an appropriately idiosyncratic but non-threatening bit of local color–like a general store or saloon. When she says "narrative in America." they cut inside, where Michael is sitting at a barstool, while a man, carefully chosen as to be sufficiently obvious as a local, tells him a story,

Local: Well, if you want a story, let me tell you about the time Old Man Hatterson's mule got loose, during the Veterans Day parade. The damn thing walks right up to the mayor's stand, while he's making his speech, and what happens? The mule takes a dump, right there and then.

Michael: (laughs heartily, while making a careful note in a notebook) Well, I can certainly see that. Now, what about your wife?

Cut to Michael actually being interviewed.

Michael: Well, Wendy, I'm really interested in how the stories people tell reflect the way they interpret and understand reality. You know– (self-consciously realizes how pretentious it all must sound) then wrapped up with humorous and self-deprecating quote, the one thing people will remember from the entire segment) Basically, it's all an excuse to be a snoop, of course.

Wendy: Ha, ha. (starts talking back at the audience, summing everything up in an easy to understand and completely inaccurate way) Michael Thomas is a collector, but what he collects are not baseball cards, or records, or paintings. He is a collector of stories. And he is certainly willing to go the ends of the earth to add a new one. And sometimes, he'll have a whole new story to add to his collection, his own transcontinental journey in search of... Narrative in America. Back to you, Jim.

Michael reflected that his entire exercise showed the narratives he had grown up with–television, non-fictional– were in their own way, just as unreal and fantastic as *Gulliver's Travels*, or *The Lord of the Rings*. He also reflected that the entire news spot said nothing about narrative in the Gold Rush country, but only commented on the style of a major metropolitan news program. Appreciating this bit of irony, he disposed of the entire fantasy, making a mental note to worry at some point about that observation's implications for his goal, and began to look for a place to stop for the night.

The next day, Michael wondered what Virginia Woolf would have done if she had moved or been born in America. He imagined her writing a novel about baseball:

```
    'I see a ball' said Jose, 'it is like a mothball by
the moonlight.
    'I hear the roar of the crowd' said Mark, 'like the
sound of a vast timorous beast awakening itself.'
    'I smell the fresh turf,' said Carney, 'and taste
peanuts and crackerjacks.'
    'I can hit fifty home runs and steal fifty bases in a
year,' said Jose 'I should be paid 3 and a half million
dollars.'
    'The men repeat the rites of spring, like the re-
blooming of flowers' said Walt.
    'I will play shortstop,' said Lance, 'and if I can
put forth and produce, Tony our manager, will make me an
everyday starter.'
    'The ball fell in between the players like a moth
which flew to close to a guttering candle,' said Carney,
'and two base-runners scored.'
```

Michael considered that it was probably a good thing Virginia Woolf had lived in England all her life.

While he was in Nevada, Michael considered the film version of his book/novel/guide. He imagined it directed by various directors.

Tristram Shandy occupied his mind between Topeka and Des Moines. He reflected that if *Narrative in America* had been written by Lawrence Sterne, he would have never left the driveway:

```
I got into my Mazda 626 blue sedan. Before I get in,
I must tell you a little bit about the car. It was
purchased in 1983 by my mother in Palo Alto
California, or actually, in Menlo Park as we lived in
Palo Alto, or actually, we at that time lived in
unincorporated land owned by Stanford University,
which had its own post office, Stanford, but was not
legally a town, thus, for practical purposes, we
always told people we were from Palo Alto, unless
they had for some reason to have a reason to have
heard of Stanford University, in which case it made
more sense to say from Stanford, which reminds me of
my uncle Henry, who at one point attempted to...
```

And so forth.

Michael knew that he belonged to a very small group of Americans whose lives were narratively structured by European literature of the past three centuries. Because European literature, in its history, gradually reached a point of questioning the possibility of narrative itself, it meant that his own life had a peculiar problem in that, to choose an example, people's whose lives were extrapolated from late seventies sitcoms or Harlequin romances didn't have. Their narratives rarely questioned their own foundation.

Michael tried to come up with a sitcom that questioned its own premises relentlessly, but failed miserably.

Moving on, we skip over the summer of 1990, when I worked quite a lot on The Fallen Ones, *but not on my own writing. I wrote several short stories during my final year at UC Santa Cruz, most of which are collected in* Something Interesting to Read, *but not the following.*

"Conversations with a Madman" is something I wrote during my last year at UC Santa Cruz; my "writer in residence" year, as my mother called it, when I was fortunate enough to live in the Merrill Guest Suites with a room-mate who was only there three nights a week. I included it in Andy Warhol's Sister *but not* Something Interesting to Read. *It's an odd piece, and always makes me feel a bit insane when I read it. I left it out of SITR because it just didn't feel like enough of a story to me. However, I think it probably should be included here for the sake of posterity and completeness.*

Excerpts From a Conversation With a Madman

Before we begin, I should say, I don't know what to call you–

Call me the madman. It is no more than I deserve.

Fine, then. Now, madman, what is it exactly that makes you mad?

I have been mad since the day I was born–I could no more be sane, than I could fly.

It's interesting you bring up flying–do you believe yourself capable of flight?

No.

Could you elaborate?

I have never, at any time, believed myself to be able to leave the earth under my own power.

If I were to say that I believe you to think yourself as a flyer, what would be your reaction?

I would think you were mad.

I am not mad, though. Define madness, please.

Madness asserts itself in your associations with other human beings—a man alone cannot be defined as a madman. I was not mad before you walked into this room.

But I did walk in. Madman, you made reference to being alone.

I did.

What makes you so alone? After all, there are voices.

Voices? I don't understand.

Let us pretend that you are the interviewer, and I am the madman.

All right. What makes you mad?

I am mad because I am with another person.

But are you mad, or do you just think you're mad?

I think I am mad because I am mad.

At what point does your madness become madness in deed, instead of just madness of thought?

My madness is purely in the head. I do things which others consider sane, but do them for reasons which are mad.

I believe we should end this game.

Do you find the game tiresome?

I believe we should end the game because it is not a game. It is real.

Perhaps you only say that because you are mad.

You mentioned voices.

I am never alone. I hear voices.

Did the voices mention this game?

What game are you speaking of?

The game in which we change places. I become you, and you become me.

I am me. The voices told me that.

Only madmen hear voices.

I am only a madman in the game, which you wished to end.

The voices are not part of the game.

I have no further questions.

Last time–
Last time.
I thought things didn't go well. I apologize.
Do you have any questions?
I'd like to begin with your childhood.
When I was a child, I could never imagine my future.
And now? You are now in what was the future to the child.
Now, I can not imagine my past.
You can't remember your past?
No. I can remember many things. However, I can not imagine a place, a situation, a world, in which such things could happen.
And then you went mad?
It was a symptom of madness, but not the cause.
A symptom?
When I became mad, my ability to imagine reality suffered.
Let us return to your childhood.
Fine.
Were you happy?
I gave great thought to the question of happiness and also sadness.
To what conclusion?
I suffered. I enjoyed. Or, I thought about both. As a child, it seemed that thinking about happiness could bring about happiness.
Did it?
It brought madness.
Now we are getting somewhere.
On the contrary, we are getting nowhere.
And this is your goal?
You ask the questions, therefore you provide the goal.
My goal is a greater appreciation of the type and quality of your madness.

I might argue you out of your goal.

You would then, I believe, have a purpose.

An anti-purpose, perhaps. A purpose to obviate the purposefulness of another.

Is such an attitude another aspect of your madness?

Possibly. Perhaps it is the cause.

You admit the possibility of a cause?

Yes.

I have no further questions.

In the spring of 1990 an event occurred which had a significant influence on my writing career—my equivalent, perhaps, of Bob Dylan first hearing Woody Guthrie or The Beatles taking LSD—I first read "The Master & Margarita" by Mikhail Bulgakov. I'd never read anything like it, full of manic energy and sunset grandeur, a mix of mischief, romance, and elegy. The novel depicted a fallen world that temporarily became epic, an idea that fit in with my mood during that strange, quiet spring, as I recovered from the emotional tumult of the previous two years.

I remained obsessed with The Master & Margarita for my remaining time in Santa Cruz. My final year at UCSC I tried adapting it as a screenplay several times, in very different ways. Since I've restricted this volume of the Complete Works to prose only, I won't include those efforts (they may show up in another volume somewhere down the line) but I will give you this excerpt from another attempt I made to rewrite the book in my own image.

Helen of Troy *was an attempt to set the story at UCSC, and somehow also involve the other major feminine presence of Goethe's* Faust, *Helen of Troy, another literary work I had become fascinated with, partly because it was such a big influence on*

Bulgakov. (I probably don't need to remind you that I named the main female character in the Notes For a Future Novel *Helen.)*

If you know anything about the novel M&M, you can see that Helen of Troy *is just a transposition of it into the key of Santa Cruz. It's basically an act of homage, and nothing more, but still fun to read, I hope.*

Duel Between the Professor and the Cowboy

In the front row of a Stevenson classroom sat a ridiculously tall man. He was thin, and seemed as if he would bend like a willow in the wind. On his head rested a vast Stetson hat, which seemed far more solid than his body. He wore brown leather, and his long legs were half swallowed by shiny boots.

Gwendolyn Margaret, associate professor of German literature at UCSC, stood before the class, lecturing on her favorite work of literature, Goethe's *Faust*–favorite because it provided the most fertile grounds for her recontextualizations.

"Mephistopheles, we can see, is a representation of the tension in Faust between the two poles of his dialectic. His inability to think outside of the masculine mode dooms him to conjure a physical representation of his own neuroses."

The tall man smiled at each statement by the professor as if it were a private joke intended solely for his benefit. After her last point, he raised his hand. The professor broke off, and indicated him with the chalk in her right hand. "You have a question?"

The man nodded and smiled graciously. He looked around at the entire class, smirking conspiratorially. The students stared back, unsure what to think. One of two, wiser than the rest, smiled back.

"Yes, yes, I do, I do. Am I to understand-" and he broke off with a small piercing laugh, as if everything were too amusing for his own comprehension. He settled his features and continued. "Am I to understand, that you do not believe the devil to be real?"

Scattered laughter greeted this truly absurd question. "I'm not sure what you mean," Gwendolyn said once the laughter died down.

"Well, well..." and a small snicker. "I mean, you think Mephistopheles was just a part of Faust's mind?"

"Well, he's a literary figure–Faust is literature, not reality. Certainly, Goethe never claims that any of this actually happened."

"Yes, yes, literature, ," the man said, as if the question of literature were entirely beside the point. He closed one eye, and the other lurched from the professor, to the students, and back to her. The professor was about to begin lecturing again when he cackled: "I was there, you know." He laughed.

"Excuse me?"

"I was there, there. I saw it all." The man began talking to the entire class. "I'll tell you, Mephisto was no 'representation of tension!'" The man's laugh became a shriek. "No, not a 'figure' at all. Very real. Real, real! More real than most of you!"

The professor's mouth opened. She looked down at her notes, but they dealt only with Mephistopheles and the bargain with the devil as a literary trope, not as a real, living entity that one could eat, drink and converse with. She looked up again, and the absurd man was still there, looking at her again with both eyes–one green, one blue. He grinned widely, revealing that one tooth was an outrageously hooked fang.

She smiled and thought of a way out of the potentially embarrassing situation: "Perhaps you'd like to discuss this during my office hours?"

"No, not all. There is nothing to discuss. You simply need to learn that the devil is real–and much closer than you think!"

Why hadn't she realized from the start that this visitor was clearly mad? Gwendolyn thought to herself. She decided that she had to retake control of the class from this obnoxious and unpleasant intruder, for it was obvious that he was not an enrolled student. "I'm afraid I can't waste any more class time with this issue–if you must talk about it, come to my office hours–"

The man's voice cut in, high and keening. "I am afraid that no more class time can be wasted with your absurd reading of Goethe's Faust. "

The professor stood straight, shocked. She was about to ask the man to leave when an excruciating pain blossomed in her breast. She gasped and dropped the chalk from her fingers, which shattered on the grey floor.

The class's TAs, who sat together on the side, rose as one and went to her side. She sat weakly, dazed, entirely forgetting what she was doing in the room. Of course, there was a general commotion.

One of the TAs yelled "Get a doctor!"

Another: "Get some water"

And more and more. "Give her air!"

"Call an ambulance!"

These helpful comments were followed by many more, less helpful but still very well intentioned. Despite all of the help, the professor was able to recover her senses somewhat, and sit in one of the chairs in the front row, nodding yes to the questions.

Ten minutes later, once Gwendolyn's health and composure had been restored with water and conversation, someone thought to ask if the man remained, and if he could be held responsible for harassment, "maybe even sexual harassment" one of the female TAs suggested. A brief inspection of the classroom and the area outside showed that the man was nowhere to be seen.

But of the nearly one hundred students in the class, not one could remember when the man had left, or how.

Once I graduated from college in June 1991 I began a somewhat aimless and peripatetic period of my life, like many young people do once they are freed from the structure that education provides them, assuming they are fortunate enough to be from economic circumstances that allows them to, of course.

I went to Europe, then spent the rest of the summer bouncing between my father's house in Palo Alto and my mother's place in Berkeley. In retrospect, I wish I had done more writing, but I didn't feel much inspiration. That's a common problem I've had in my life—whenever I have nothing to do but write, I don't tend to be very productive. On the other hand, when I have a full-time job that I actually care about, I don't write much either since I devote all of my energy to it. The optimal mix seems to be to do part or even full-time I don't care about that much, which leaves me enough energy to write but takes up enough time that whatever I have leftover I value more. That's not unusual, really—think of all the part-time workers in LA who are trying to make it as screenwriters, actors, comedians, etc.—but it took me a long time to figure out it was true for myself. It also shows that it would have been disastrous if I had become independently wealthy while working in tech, because although I fantasized about doing nothing but writing once I had my IPO winnings, I probably would have spent all of my time squandering my fortune in the most expeditious manner possible, like Jack Aubrey on shore.

In the fall of '91 I started temping, which was good because it got me out of the house, and into some money. A usual day was for me would be to work a full day at my temp job, then head to my father's office afterward. In 1990 my father had started a consulting company, which had a nice office in a new building in downtown

Menlo Park, located above the famous bookstore Kepler's Books. I would buy coffee at Café Borrone, and go up to the office; ostensibly to write, but often I would just play SimCity until late in the night.

After the lively intensity and intense sociality of my life in Santa Cruz, returning to suburbia was a big change. I started thinking about my past, and about artistic inspiration, since I felt I lacked it. I wondered if I really had the drive to be an artist, if I wanted it enough. I was haunted by these lyrics by Neil Peart, from Rush's 1987 album "Hold Your Fire"

> *"When I feel the powerful visions, their fire made alive*
> *I wish I had that instinct – I wish I had that drive"*

I was caught somewhere between wanting and wanting to want, feeling stuck, dreaming of writing something truly great, but not able to actually sit down and do it. I did write a few fragments, including the following selection is that classic writerly exercise, writing about writing block. It's about as exciting as it sounds. I find it funny to read now, because it's such a young person's idea of what being old is like.

"Fragment"

Throughout that cold, lonely autumn, he tried to find inspiration, and avoid the dark cliché that came to his mind, that the time of nature's barrenity was also the time of his decline. What had happened? he wondered. When had the promise of the previous year turned to the pointless perambulations of the new?

He read over the journal entry made that morning:

```
Woke early, went back to sleep. Even writing those
words exhaust me. I have been typing these entries
now for a month, perhaps I should go back to writing
by hand. I don't think it's any different anyway, and
I find it disturbing to have my most unformed
thoughts set down in formal type, as if giving them a
status they neither enjoy nor deserve. Perhaps I
flatter myself.

No, no. I just looked back on that last thought, and
reject it utterly. There are good reasons for typing,
the real problem lies elsewhere.
```

After he looked at the two paragraphs, he could not remember what had inspired him to take either position in his mind. He tossed the page aside and went into the kitchen to fix a drink.

Staring out the window, holding the trembling glass, a sentence began to form in his mind. 'The moss underfoot seemed to glisten...' He held on to the word, 'glisten.' It had been so long since he thought of a word like that .

But what could be done with it? He found no joy of creation in the juxtaposition of moss with glisten–it seemed like such a hopeless bid for artistry. Possibly the ice could glisten, but... what the devil was the use?–he was describing nothing, it was all happening in a vacuum. Moss or ice, it made no difference, because there were no people in whatever he was describing. They were just words, words he tested together in the laboratory of his mind. All that inspired him was the momentary appearance of a word he had not thought of in a great while.

Perhaps a poem...

The moss lay glistening
Not flat as moss usually is.

No.

Some hours later he went for a walk. The utter flatness of everything exhausted him. With him he brought an elegant notebook an acquaintance had bought him in Italy. He carried it awkwardly, as a man unused to children would carry an infant.

The trees were dark green, the sky light blue. The snow lay in un-variegated bundles by the path, surrounded by patches of a flattened dirt-grass mixture.

In his mind he tried to remember his wife in Paris. It had been almost too many years ago. What was it she had always said at that certain restaurant?

"I think you love your pen more than your penis-" Then she had laughed, lowly and deeply. That was after he had stayed up all night to finish the first part of *The Memoirs of the Magnificent Conjurer.*

At that time had taken pride and pleasure in her joke. Now he wondered if she had been mocking him, laying the seeds of their separation, carefully yet casually laying evidence for the future. It was not Paris that lay most heavily on his mind, though, but New Jersey. Late November.

When he arrived back at the small cottage he had rented from the university, he went to the typewriter and struck the keys slowly.

```
I thought of my wife during my walk. She told me I
loved my pen more than my penis. What was once funny
to me is now bitter. My thoughts become more clichéd
the older I get. Once again everything is interpreted
through the mist of my autumnal misery.
```

He pushed the typewriter to the back of the desk. It was already dark.

Very late in 1991, my writer's block started to crumble and I began writing new material for Notes For a Future Novel—*on December 22ⁿᵈ, apparently, judging by the entry in my*

MacNovelCount excel file, which I used to track how much I was writing for NFFN in a bizarrely obsessive fashion. I found it very motivating to keep track of how many words I was writing, and how many I averaged per day. If only National Novel Writing Month had existed back then!

I left my temp job in January 1991, having saved enough money that I didn't need to work again for a while. I resolved to concentrate on writing, and indeed, I spent most of the next year and a half working on NFFN. However, I also started a few other pieces when inspiration struck me.

The first of these is "One Setback After Another," from the spring of 1992. This story was inspired by living with my father and watching his attempts to manage communications with my ex-step-mother, whom he had divorced the previous year. This story is set during a curious transition period in communication technologies, just before the widespread adoption of the Internet but when fax machines were sufficiently prevalent that they allowed asynchronous communication by the printed page, like a very primitive form of email.

One Setback After Another

He worked on the fax for hours, weighing each word and measuring the phrases. It was his new theory that she would read only the first question, so the rest were irrelevancies, made up simply to take up space and give her the illusion that if she were too busy to deal with all his concerns at least she could do one.

The questions he finally settled on were:

```
1) What are the arrangements for Thanksgiving? I need
to know two things: first if you are coming out here,
```

```
and if so, precise dates and times of arrival and
departure of the boys so I can make plane
reservations.
```

This, in the most precise terms he could muster, was the matter that he was desperate to have answered.

The other four questions were crafted to seem important enough so she wouldn't realize they were irrelevant, yet imprecise and vague enough that if by some mischance she should deal with them, no untoward ramifications could develop:

```
2) I need a list of ideas for my mother and sisters
to buy Christmas presents.
3) We need to deal with Bradley and David's
portfolios.
4) We need to begin thinking about the summer of next
year.
5) I think Bradley could use more white socks.
```

He nodded, satisfied with these questions. He tapped in her auto-dial code on the fax machine, the top one, and shoved it in the narrow slit in the side.

The matter went unresolved for several days. It was depressing, it seemed now he must expend effort on confirming her reception of the fax, instead of getting the response he desired. His usual strategy in such situations was to first speak to the family member that he still had the most contact with—her father, Bradley and David's maternal grandfather.

In his office that evening, during the time he set aside each night to deal with the seemingly irresolvable difficulty of his plans for Thanksgiving, he dialed the code for her parents on his office phone system.

"Hello?" he said when the receiver was picked up on the other side. There was a brief silence. Finally:

"Hello," a woman said in doubtful tones.

"Hi, I'd like to speak to L–?"

This was a common difficulty at her parents' house, a never-ending succession of different people answering the phone. There was never the sense of a comfortable routine in communicating with L–, or with his daughter for that matter.

"I think... no, wait..." The receiver emitted no sound for some seconds, he guessed that a hand had gone over the receiver. Then he heard troubled wheezing.

"I'm sorry... what did you say your name was?"

"Dudley Mihailoff."

"I see... are you sure you have the right number? Actually..." and it seemed to him that there was a whole committee dealing with the matter on the other side discussing the matter.

"Is this 343-9080?" he said. There was no reply. He could hear multiple disembodied voices floating beyond the phone. Occasional words like what, L–, coincidence, and aware crossed the barrier but formed no coherent sentence.

"Hello?" the woman's voice, a little more confident, returned.

"Yes. I'm trying to reach L— P—. Have I called at a bad time?"

"I'm sorry, we weren't sure if he was out. It turned out he was downstairs. He is here, though."

A pause. No one said anything.

"Can I talk to him?"

"Sure" the woman said brightly. "He's right here."

The line fell silent. Again he guessed that a hand had been placed over the other end. Seven minutes had passed since he dialed the number.

When it had reached ten, L— came on the line, friendly and open. "Hi, Dudley. Sorry for the wait. How are you?

"Fine. How are you?"

"The usual. What can I do for you?"

"Have you talked to Priscilla?

"Yes, just this afternoon, in fact."

"Did she mention receiving my fax?"

"No, not to me, no."

"It's just real important that I know what her plans for Thanksgiving are."

"I don't know any more than you. To be honest, I've tried asking her and gotten some very vague answers. I could try calling her then calling you back this week."

"Okay."

"We'll keep in touch."

"Okay. Thanks, bye."

At five-thirty the next morning, the fax machine emitted one piece of curly white paper. On it, scrawled in large, blurry letters were these words:

```
I already dealt with Bradley and David's portfolios,
with a broker in San Francisco. Also, I need a list
of all possible times you can be with the boys so I
can arrange schedules with my parents. Regards, P.
```

The first part was true, he had known already from talking to L—, which was why he had put in the fax–if she already had done something about it on her own she would be unlikely to respond to it. Unfortunately, she had. Perhaps it had been a mistake to mention such an important issue, no matter how likely it had seemed she would ignore it.

Now it was up to him to formulate a new strategy. L— was working on it as well, so that was one avenue, however, there should be more. He could risk a direct phone call–on these matters she usually would speak to him. It would be time consuming however, and nerve-wracking. Also, she was hard to reach and leaving a message was about thirty-three percent less effective than sending another fax. He decided to wait another twenty-four hours.

In the meantime, he wrote down what scant information he already had on her plans in a file on his notebook computer:

```
1) L— does not know her plans. They actually are
uncertain, instead of her refusing to tell me.
2) She told me during a phone call I could see them
for two days during Thanksgiving, Sat. and Sun.
3) Since then I have read in the newspaper her
husband's co. is launching a new drug during the
first week of Dec.
4) Bradley told me "mommy wants to go away" for
Thanksgiving.
```

It seemed to him at this point that all the signs pointed to her coming out, except for the first, which was the biggest objection. It was possible that she would come out but not visit her parents, but this was extremely unlikely, and he only considered it because his attempt to make a coherent list was floundering so badly.

He could not give up. His options were narrowing, however, it was without a doubt that once he used a stratagem, it would be ignored henceforth. In front of him was an invitation to speak at the Institute for National Policy Affairs in Washington DC; whether he accepted or not depended on his plans for Thanksgiving.

He wished L— would call, his best luck interfacing with her was usually through her father. However, when he returned to his house at six that evening, there was no answering machine message of importance.

He set down his briefcase. He took out his frequent flyer guide and opened to the page that contained the flights from San Francisco to New York City. He had to face it, he must attempt a direct phone call.

He dialed #1, the code on his phone machine for her home number.

The phone was answered after the first ring, For a second he could not believe his good fortune, until he noticed something curious, a mechano-electronic click, followed by her voice–but obviously recorded. "Hi, you've reached the Gerald residence. We can't come to the phone right now. If this is a business call for Jeremy Gerald–"

Her new husband–he obviously received business calls at home, which she definitely would not like–yet another sign of their incompatibility.

"Please press one. If it is a personal call for Jeremy Gerald, please press two. If it is a personal call for Priscilla Gerald, please press three. If it is a call dealing with household matters, please press four. If you have reached this number by accident, please press five."

He decided his call was personal for Priscilla and pressed three. He heard various electronic hums, tones and beeps through the receiver. Then:

"Hi, this is Priscilla. I'm not available right now. If you would like to speak to my husband Jeremy, please press one. If you would like to speak to one of the household staff, please press two. If you would like to leave a message for me, please press three and speak at the tone. If it is an emergency concerning Bradley or David, please dial four, and you will be connected to my emergency child-pager."

Although he was intrigued by the fourth option, he knew it would be egregious violation of their mutual understanding to use it. He decided to try Jeremy, whom he was friendly with.

After another sequence of mysterious electronic noises, he reached another message, all of which, he observed, were made by Priscilla–obviously, she had insisted on the system as part of their new household.

"Jeremy's not available right now. If you would like to leave a message for him, press one. If you would like to be connected to a member of the household staff, press two."

He decided to try two. Perhaps they were out and Bradley and David were being taken care of by a babysitter.

He heard a synthetic trill, which meant the phone was ringing. He let it ring ten times, but no one ever picked up. He kept expecting to hear a prompt to leave a voicemail, but he never got one and finally he hung up. Another dead-end.

The phone rang, broke him out of a deep sleep, and he answered, fearing the worst. "Hello." He heard a faint electronic tone but no human voice. "Hello? Hello?"

A voice came on, sounding like Priscilla. "Hi, Dad, this is Priscilla–

"Prisc–" Her voice continued rudely, not recognizing his response in the slightest. "–I hope this is the right hotel room."

"Priscilla?" His sleep-addled mind could not function–why was she calling at three-thirty in the morning, why did she call him 'dad' and why didn't she stop?

"I think September 5th is fine for us. Hope you get this message. Bye."

He was a little more awake now and realized what he must have been hearing, Priscilla and Jeremy's new phone system contained some sort of auto-callback function, a kind of pre-emptive voicemail, and a message had been scheduled to be sent to him–one that had actually been meant for her father.

L—— must have been in some far eastern time zone, most likely Europe since the message had been delivered at a time that would have been unforgivably rude had he been at home or on the east coast.

That raised the disturbing yet plausible possibility, that meant that there was a message somewhere meant for him which had gotten lost; maybe switched, maybe last night or this morning, L— was going to get the one meant for him. He must get in touch with him and prevent this looming catastrophe.

Considering all of this, he got little sleep the rest of the night, especially since the birds seemed very loud just before sunset.

In re-reading the story some two decades later I am surprised to find myself filled with nostalgia for my ex-step-mother's family. Not to ethnically stereotype, by which I mean I will now engage in ethnic stereotyping, but they were a classic Jewish family, which would spend nearly every weekend gathering, either at one of the offspring houses in Palo Alto, or at the grand-parents' house in Mill Valley. They seemed to actually enjoy each other's company, an interesting revelation for a kid from a very WASP-y family.

Though things ended badly, I do remember a lot of good times at their house in Mill Valley, and ex-step-mother's father, in particular was a good and kind man, a mensch, if you will indulge me in some appropriation of Jewish culture. He called my sister and me his "acquired" grand-children since he thought "step" had too many negative connotations. Sadly he died not too many years after I composed this piece. I believe that lingering response may explain why I didn't make up a fictional name for him, but instead used the very 19th century trick of eliding the name with the first letter and then a string of dashes.

This is probably one of the few times I ever tried to write something from the point of view of a character based on a family member. The title was directly taken from something my father sometimes say at times of maximum frustration, usually due to travel friction or offspring-originated giznank, like a late arrival at Lake Shasta or inappropriate personal items brought on a camping trip.

Although amusing, I think it finally became too uncomfortable to continue, and that may still be true, given the fact that I failed in my attempt to finish it during the preparation of this collection. So, instead of writing from the thinly fictionalized point of view of a family member I went back to Notes For a Future Novel and what I knew best—writing from my own, thinly fictionalized point of view.

Two bits of name-related trivia: the story did give me the names that I used for my half-brother analogues in the Santa Zita trilogy—they appear in an early chapter of 1989 A Novel, *an outtake that will probably appear in the special expanded edition I plan to release in 2034 in honor of that novel's twentieth anniversary (kidding! I think.) The other is that I used the last name "Mihailoff" for Dudley, which was the last name I used for Tim for a while. (I suppose these two facts imply that "One Setback After Another" takes place in the Zitaverse, though I never explicitly mention Tim.)*

It's a name in my family tree which I appropriated because I liked its Russian-ness, but later thought better of and came up with the more fictional "Page" which I thought was a better choice because it was so generic and Anglo-Saxony, like Hall, and because I liked the associations with the idea of books and textuality, in that Tim is sort of a tabula rasa, *if you will.*

Between 1991 and 1993 I became moderately obsessed with grunge rock, my generation's (the white, middle class part, at least) one indisputable contribution to western civilization. As depicted in the 1992 romantic comedy Singles, *Seattle beckoned to me like a GenX city on the hill, an earthly paradise of cool clubs, artsy cafes, cute girls in black tights and flowery miniskirts, and flannel clad rockers, where you could just stroll into a club on a random Tuesday night and see Pearl Jam, Alice In Chains, Screaming Trees, or some new band that was going to be even more revelatory and generation defining.*

Because I wrote this before I had actually moved there, there isn't really a lot of local detail in it. Instead, it's mainly interesting because it's me imagining what it would be like to be in a rock band, without actually knowing anything about it, beyond the third hand descriptions in magazines like Rolling Stone, Spin and BAM. I had hung around musicians a fair amount in my first few years at Santa Cruz, but not even a tincture of musicianship had penetrated my consciousness.

Mourningfuck

"He's the lead singer of Mourningfuck," one girl said.

"Really?" replied the other.

I heard these words behind me. I didn't turn around, pretending not to hear. I smiled at the woman behind the counter. I could get used to this.

"Excuse me," the first girl said, the words now directed towards me. Now I looked. I saw the two girls. Since I wasn't wearing my contacts, they appeared as two blond smudges in pink sweaters.

"Are you Johnny Zach, from Mourning... you know?" she broke off, seemingly overcome by shyness.

"Fuck? Yeah," I said, chuckling.

"We saw you at the club. You guys were awesome."

She sounded young, maybe still in high school. If word of us was passing around high school, something must be happening.

I smiled. It's hard to smile when you can't really see the person's face that you're smiling at. For some reason I didn't want to wear glasses that day. I like not being able to see someone's face. I knew Jane, the woman at the counter, so I didn't need to see her in detail. Walking around and seeing the world all fuzzy made me feel stoned.

I moved to Seattle to go to school. I lasted at U-Dub for about three months, but I at least made some friends before my complete lack of interest in academia made it necessary I drop out. I kept up with those friends. They all played in bands. They asked me if I could play.

I had an acoustic guitar I'd dicked around with in high school. Peter (the guy with the bass) had actually played in a real band, so I was pretty psyched to be jamming with him. Funny, but he actually liked playing with me. He told me I knew the right chords, without having to be told.

I went home for Christmas, and it wasn't any better than it had been for the first eighteen years I spent there. On the day after New Year's, I found myself driving back to Seattle for the beginning of school, even though I had been told in no uncertain terms that I wasn't ever going to be a student there again.

Pete let me crash in his dorm room for two weeks. Hid is more like it. I slept in his closet, and only came out when the RA was at class. It got a little crowded, between Pete, me, his roommate and Pavement. Pavement was Pete's girlfriend (sort of.) More about her, later. I spent almost a week, drinking beer to pass the time and pissing in a 32-ounce Sprite bottle. Every day, Pete would make me jam with him. He started calling me 'Johnny.' Everyone had always called me John in my family. I liked 'Johnny.' It wasn't really me, and yet, it sort of fit, because I didn't really have any kind of a life.

Pete had the ability, which I didn't, of being able to party all the time, and still just get by in his classes. After a while, the RA got wise and I had to move out. I still had some money saved, so I got a dirt-cheap place, a pit, near school. I got a job and lost touch with Pete for a few months.

I need to tell you about Pavement, I guess. Everyone always asks about her name. Some women find it really offensive when they hear Pete call her that. He didn't start it, though. He met her through a friend of a friend of a friend. Pete is one of those guys who's just really connected. We've traveled together, and he always knows someone, or knows of someone, in just about every city in this land. He's not superficial, he just seems to have this instinct.

When I met Pete, Pavement was his girlfriend. She was really a trip. She loved music. I think she came over to Pete's room because he has such an awesome collection of LPs. Actually, I listened to his records a lot, too. He had good taste. I grew up in Temperance, a small town in eastern Washington. Zeppelin, Skynyrd, Floyd, were what me and my friends listened too. Over and over. I've actually told people about my memories of getting stoned in the high school parking lot, listening to an 8-track tape of Black Sabbath, and had them look at me as if I had been one of the signers of the Declaration of Independence. I can't believe my shitty little small town life is now public property, something that other people might find incredible and cool. Anything can be romanticized is the only conclusion I can draw.

Back to Pavement, though. My first impression was of a very thin, possibly anorectic (but it turns out she just didn't eat a lot) girl, lying on her back, listening to the Velvet Underground and singing along in a creepy, quavering falsetto, like a demon-possessed child. I thought she was crazy, and not in a good way, but actually mentally ill.

For two weeks she wouldn't talk to me. We would hang out while Pete went to class, both drinking Old Milwaukee, listening to records. She chose them. I liked her choices, so I never tried to do it myself. Every so often I would say something like "I really like this band/ song/ album/ type of weather" or something that seemed friendly, but not intended to trigger further conversation. Instead, she would smile at me and go back to her world. Eventually, I stopped talking to her and just listened. I discovered she was the kind of girl you could be quiet with and have it not be awkward.

I think it was some kind of test. Suddenly, she started talking to me. I was extremely attracted to her. Before I met Pavement, I'd never met a girl without feathered hair in person. Her hair was thin, long and straight. She dyed it with henna, a process that she once inflicted on Pete and I.

The bands she liked were the Beatles, Velvet Underground, early Pink Floyd (stuff I had no idea existed. I thought their first album was *Dark Side of the Moon*. That was what my friend in Temperance told me.) James Brown, the Bryds, the Grateful Dead, but only their first album.

Most of the time, Pete, Pavement and I sat around, drank beers and shot the shit—mostly about music. It wasn't until I was working, a few months later, I realized Pete wasn't fooling around when were hanging out. In a roundabout way, he was telling me we should start a band. He never said it. He just got my ideas on music, told me his, and played. The only clue was that he started calling me "Johnny."

There was a cafe around the corner. One night I ran into Pavement there. I saw her out of the corner of my eye and was tempted not to say hi to her. She, though, saw me and instantly came over. She told me Pete was hanging out nearby. She told me to go.

I showed up. Pete was there, with three other guys. They were jamming. Pete handed me a guitar and launched into "Sweetleaf." This was a song I had played with Pete. But now, it was me and another guitarist. That was the night Mourningfuck was born.

It was weird. Pete could really play guitar. He would play all this really complicated stuff and I would try to keep up, playing easy bass chords on an acoustic guitar. Every so often he would stop and seem really into what I had just played. He'd be like: "Johnny, excellent. Perfect." He didn't seem to care about his own playing, and if I returned his compliments, he just kind of shrugged. He told me he liked the way my notes went with his. What could I tell them? I was just playing what anyone would play?

About a week of jam sessions later, Pete suddenly said: "You are a bassist." We went into his room. He fucked around with his stereo and put on Led Zeppelin II. When it played, I realized Pete had twisted the knobs so the only thing you could hear was the deep throb of John Paul Jones's bass.

"Listen" he told me. We listened to all of Led Zeppelin II like this–just a muffled, droning pulse of pure bass. Pete pulled out the bong and we got stoned. When the record finished, Pete put it on again. I asked him if what we were doing was okay for the stereo. He said it didn't matter.

Pavement said: "Put on Sergeant Pepper's." Pavement would talk when I was around, and even use my name, but still would never speak directly to me. We ended up listening to Led Zeppelin II three times, all the way through. By the third time through side two, I was so stoned I fell asleep on the floor, staring at the speakers and imagining I could see them vibrating to the music. When I woke up, it was morning and both Pavement and Pete were gone. (I found out later that they, logically enough, had decided to have sex in my bed since I had sort of crashed in their room. Amazingly, my roommate slept through the whole thing.)

Maybe this is just my warped perspective, but there was a basic problem with Pete and Pavement's relationship. She loved music more than anything, and wanted to be with Pete because he made music that she considered an equal of the records she loved so much. Pete, though, wanted to be loved for him. With anyone else, he was satisfied if they idealized him as a musician–it was all part of the plan–but he wanted Pavement to see him as a normal person. She couldn't, though. She just didn't think that way.

One of Pete's many ways of keeping out jam sessions unpredictable was to have us suddenly jam on some song which all of us sort of knew but really didn't. Songs we'd heard on the radio but would never think of actually learning. He had us play pop, funk and reggae, old songs, new songs, songs he confessed to us he really hated but wanted to see if it was the performance of the song he hated or the song itself. Most of the time it was a hopeless failure. I can't really play funk or reggae, I can't really play anything, to be honest. Since we were supposed to be a hard rock band, it was weird that we played this stuff, but Pete had all these reasons why. He said Keith Richards loved reggae, that James Brown was John Bonham's favorite artist of all time. He wanted us to have all these different grooves in our heads, to feel them. He said the only way to play hard rock right was to play it like it was something else.

Like a lot of stuff Pete had us do, I could never tell if it helped us or not. I think, ultimately, it was a good idea, but sometimes, as we lumbered through the worst versions of 'Mrs. Robinson' 'Lively Up Yourself' and 'I Wish' that I have ever been performed in the history of mankind, I had to wonder it wasn't all a practical joke on Pete's part.

I realize another important thing about this story is that I used the first person for the first time since college. First person was such a cliché among young writers when I was at UCSC that I shied away from it, so turned off by the sub-Holden Caulfield efforts of my creative writing classmates. Everything I wrote for NFFN and the Santa Zita novels was in the third person, up until 2003, when I tried the first person as an experiment when I was feeing stuck in Celebrated Summer.

I had been advised to do by my writing teacher at the time, Tom Barbash, who suggested that if you felt stuck writing from a character's point of view, not just describing the action but trying to give a clue to a character's emotional state via the description, it can be useful to try writing in first person, then later convert it to third.

I discovered I liked writing in first, and when I did NaNoWriMo in November 2004, I wrote it in first person. By that point I felt confident and experienced enough that I could in first without falling into the clichés or the traps that befall the lazy writer, such as too much introspections and too many internal monologues; forgetting to describe anything and having the character obsess about what to do next, instead of just doing it. More accurately, I let myself fall into those traps, confident that I could remove and rewrite the bad writing once I moved onto the next draft.

At the end of the summer of 1993, I made the mistake of moving to Seattle and discovered that it was like some of the cool parts of the Bay Area combined with a hopelessly provincial, culturally backward metropolis that still lived and died on the fortunes of two companies, Boeing and Microsoft. The reason that Seattle had so many great bands had been an accident of history, the fact that a few very talented people happened to be born in Washington state at the same time, there happened to be enough clubs for a while to support a scene, and the shitty weather and the lack of things to do meant that the bands had little else to do other than practice.

Demonstrating that, perhaps, was my own level of focus and productivity while I was living there. As a result, there are actually no extant out-takes or unfinished projects from my eight months there. I started writing The Deep and Savage Way soon after I arrived, and I finished the first draft just before I left. I hadn't been so focused and dedicated to a project since Therapy during my last *year at Santa Cruz. Shows you what you can accomplish when you are depressed and alone, I guess.*

Once I returned from Seattle in April 1994, I was consumed with the desire to find my next big project. I really, really wanted to write something that was as compelling to me as *Therapy* or *DSW*. I was still amazed at myself for writing an entire novel while I was living in Seattle, and I was eager to feel that sense of achievement again.

The most natural thing was for me to write the next volume of the *Santa Zita Stories*, so that's what I did. Unlike *DSW*, though, this turned out to be mostly a reclamation project–taking the passages of *NFFN* that were written from Helen's point of view, changing "Santa Cruz" to "Santa Zita" and then adding new material when I felt moved to. I titled this work, somewhat unimaginatively, Helen of Santa Zita.

My memory is hazy but fortunately I save (almost) everything, so I was able to find a draft dated Nov. 7, 1994, so apparently I was working on it all the way from when I finished the first draft of *DSW* in early 1994 when I was still in Seattle, all the way to the following fall, when I was living at The Hotel in San Francisco's Lower Haight neighborhood. I thought about including that draft in this collection, but instead opted for a later, longer version from 2001, in the interests of making this book thick enough that the spine wouldn't be so narrow that I couldn't put the title in a font large enough to read.

During the winter and spring of 1995, I continued to struggle to find a new project that held my interest. For a while I worked on another installment of the Santa Zita Stories, The Great Wheel, which was going to be Tim's novel, the third in the trilogy that already included DSW and HSZ. I wrote a bunch of notes, but didn't actually write any actual text, which I now realize was a bad habit I struggled with a lot during that stage of my career, which I touched on while discussing Mrs. Faust, *in that I would spend more time preparing to write than actually doing it.*

The problem is this: outlining and note-taking can be valuable (and if you have an idea it's essential to get it down somehow) but it can easily become a substitute for Actual Writing, and once you do get to the point when you have to start composing the work, you may find that the original inspiration and energy you felt about the work has been diluted. I should have just started writing and let the book reveal itself to me that way, instead of trying to dictate it in a top-down fashion. I wonder if my experience in the tech industry had already started to subconsciously influence me, since so much software development is still driven by the classic waterfall model of concept-design-implement-debug.

A related problem was that I felt stymied in the lack of a big idea to tie it all together. By that point I had progressed beyond what I had done when writing Notes For a Future Novel, *which was to just write, with no over-arching plan or idea, other than a few literary parallels. In retrospect, it was a mistake to let the lack of a big idea stop me from writing. Instead, I should have just started writing, accumulated a mass of material, and let the idea emerge organically. The solution to every problem in writing is to write. My writing teacher Tom Barbash once told me the answers were all in the text, I just had to find them, and he was very right.*

Alas, Tom was many years in my future I was still lost in the weeds, trying to find my way. Even though I was three plus years out from being a lit student, the great works of western literature still hung over me. Having transposed Dante's Inferno into a modern setting while living in Seattle, I turned my sights to another one of my favorites from college, Goethe's Faust, *which meant, of course, that I was once again trying to rewrite The Master & Margarita in my own image, since it was impossible for me to adapt* Faust *with consciously and unconsciously having it turn into the M&M.*

In this case, it was set in a high tech company much like the ones I had been temping at in the Bay Area and Seattle from 1991 to 1994. Although this might seem odd if you think of Faust as being primarily about a man selling his soul to the devil, in fact it made a certain amount of sense. Goethe's Faust II *was, among many other things, about mankind's use of technology to make and remake the world, and the spiritual cost of such endeavors. I saw something Faustian in the famous technology executives of the time like Steve Jobs, Scott McNealy, Larry Ellison, and especially Bill Gates, in their profound faith in their own intellects, human ingenuity and desires to build totalizing systems of technology that would embrace and extend all human thought, just as Faust built an extensive system of dikes and dams to push back the sea and build a kingdom on the reclaimed land.*

The Consultant

Ted Heath, Director of USA Marketing for Xerox Computing Systems, sighed and slouched farther down in his chair stretching his legs beneath the ovular beige coffee table. He, along with the rest of the XOS 4.0 Worldwide Rollout Sales & Marketing Team, were waiting for the Consultant to arrive.

Nobody knew what their name was or why they had so suddenly been brought aboard. That morning, Ted had received an email from the EVP of Corporate Marketing, John Faust, directing them to the Gounod conference room to meet the Consultant. That's all it said: "the Consultant". No name, no explanation of who or why he would be there, what role he was to perform, or why he had been brought aboard, only two weeks to go before the XOS 4.0 rollout. And yet, here they were in the conference room, wasting time and precious departmental bandwidth, when they were already working twelve hours a day, seven days a week.

To add insult to injury to indignity, John himself, and the Consultant, were nowhere to be seen. They were half an hour late. To pass the time, Ted once again surveyed the meeting participants. Beverly Edmunds, Director of XUSA (pronounced "zoosa") Sales and Bob Garfunkel, Special Adjunct to the Vice-President, sat shifting and fidgeting in their seats. A fourth person, a marketing temp who worked with Beverly, had the most intelligent approach to the situation–he was fast asleep, Ted noted enviously, slumped in his chair, arms folded and chin resting on his black sweatshirt.

Ted reviewed the email John has sent to the Team that morning, which he had printed in order to make it more comprehensible, or to use as evidence, if it came to that. It has been waiting for them all when they got to work on the department's Xerox Computing Systems OfficeLink Pro, usually shorted to just "X-Link", a unified email, document-sharing, and database system which first had been built as an extension to XOS 3.1 by a small Seattle-based company named Microsoft. Up to that point Microsoft has only been known only as a developer of applications for a failed competitor to the Xerox Star 100, called the Apple Macintosh. It had survived, someone had told Ted at a very boring cocktail party, only because it had written the standard implementation of BASIC for the XOS that was used in most elementary and middle schools. Apparently the company's CEO was a very smart guy, since he had planned and led the development of this revolutionary software for corporate offices.

Ted was so bored he found himself recounting in his mind the whole story of John Faust and the OfficeLink acquisition. John had first made a name for himself at Xerox Computing by flying up to Seattle just after OfficeLink was released. Ted remembered, because he had been there; he was part of the team that John brought to meet with Microsoft–he brought a large team, it was part of his strategy he told Ted on the corporate jet flying up there.

The scenes of their advance into Microsoft played themselves over in Ted's mind (they often did when he woke up in the middle of the night): their march into the conference room, seeing Bill Gates, a thin, gawky man with a self-importance far behind the relative status of his company and the cool, commanding smile with which John has delivered the crushing blow: XC engineers had reverse-engineered Microsoft's code, he told Gates, and were going to build the technology into the next release of XOS. They had two choices: sell the technology to XC now for some money, or they would build it into XOS later and Microsoft wouldn't make anything. Crushed, Gates had no choice but to submit to the acquisition. The look of devastation on Gates's face was not one Ted would ever forget, and it had changed his view of John Faust from one of mere respect to a mingling of terror and awe.

Except that it was all a lie, John told Ted on the flight home. Microsoft's code was air-tight, it would have taken at least a year for them to reverse-engineer it. By bluffing, they had gotten the code for far under market value.

That had been John's greatest triumph and it led to him being placed in XC's highest circle: an executive vice-presidency. Now, however, he was seemingly poised for even greater heights. The release of XOS 4.0, an upgrade to the world's dominant operating system for personal computers that was to be much more. It was, as John continuously reminded his Team (he always capitalized that word in his communications) and the marketing department as a whole, "the most important piece of software in the history of mankind," the first step in eventually connecting every single computer in the world to a global network, a true Information Super-Highway, all powered by XC software.

It was John Faust's will that had driven the Team to put in seventy-hour weeks for six months, that had caused them to consider and debate every single detail, and to create a marketing plan that John likened to the Allied invasion of Normandy in the complexity of its logistics. It resided as a 20-megabyte file in a Xerox Galaxy 2000 server two stories beneath them, basking in perpetual 62° comfort.

And he was always present. John Faust was legendary for his complete mastery of the art of touching base. Even when he was out of the office, he was in touch, by email, voicemail, video-conference. There was no time when one of his employees could expect that he wouldn't be able to somehow contact them. Tales were told in the coffee room, about receiving an email from John when he had gone on a trip across Antarctica in a dogsled, of how he had been the first to get his email up after the '89 quake, or the time he had nearly been arrested by the Secret Service for trying to use an experimental cellular modem on Air Force One, which had caused the plane's navigation system to go haywire, and for a terrifying five minutes, convince the President's team that nuclear war had just broken out.

No matter where John Faust was, what nation, what continent, what city, he was always in touch, and could always be reached. That was a given. Even if John Faust was sent to hell itself, Ted was sure, he would send an email back; "Boy is it hot here and by the way, you're a day behind schedule orienting the VAR sales force."

But now something has gone terribly wrong. Not only was he late, which was normal, but he had made no effort to alert them as to why or when he could expected. That was definitely not normal.

Once more Ted decided to question the rest of the Team, unwilling and unable to accept that John Faust was now thirty-five minutes late and completely unaccounted for.

"Beverly," he said the to the severe, short-haired woman sitting directly across from him. She looked up with her piercing brown eyes. Everything about Beverly was sharp and angular, from her precisely defined dome of brown-blond hair to downward-sloping, pointy nose, to the long rows of the printed spreadsheet in front of her, detailing the various media buys she was responsible for. "You're sure John didn't..."

"He hasn't sent an email."

"I just can't understand it," Bob Garfunkel broke in. "I'm starting to be seriously concerned."

"I tried fingering his account, and something unusual happened." said Abraham Zinfinder, the Teams technical liaison, from far down at the other end of the conference table. "His account was temporarily frozen out, so I ran a status check using DirectSys. It's got this cool new feature—"

"Yes, yes, " interrupted Beverly. "I'm sure it's great. What happened? Did you find him?"

"No. My computer crashed," said Abraham, opened his mouth, then closed it again.

Beverly nodded as if that were exactly what she expected. Ted, though, studied Abraham's face. He seemed nervous—not the usual jittery Jolt-induced happy nervousness of a programmer, but just... nervous.

"And that's all?" Ted asked.

Abraham took a breath. "Well, no, that's not all. My computer froze. I was about to reboot when a message box popped up, saying 'Don't try that again'".

"Sounds like a computer virus," Beverly said.

"No, no, it can't have been that. My computer was frozen. The system was completely inactive. What happened was impossible."

"Did you run virus-check?"

"No."

"Why not?"

"I just... it just didn't seem like a good idea," Abraham said, and glanced quickly around him.

Beverly's eyes fell to the binder in front of her, convinced that Abraham was having them on. Ted shrugged. Whatever had happened, Abraham was reluctant to talk about it, or even to investigate. He couldn't remember another time when Abraham seemed so uninterested in solving a mysterious computer problem. Ted had once seen him spend an hour with the marketing temp, tracking down an obscure printer incompatibility just because the temp had asked him a question he couldn't answer.

Ted shook his head. What a weird morning. Seven days to rollout. Eleven-forty-five. Six and a half, almost.

He looked down at the email John had sent them:

```
To: XOS 4 Rollout Team
From: jfaust
Subject: Ten am meeting
Team -- Meet me at the Gounoud Room at ten to meet
the Consultant. Attendance is mandatory.
  --jfaust
```

Nothing more, no explanation. The more Ted studied the message the less he understood it. At that moment, he felt a chill pass through him, followed by a sinking in his stomach; a sensation of both sickness and exhilaration, as if he were in a rollercoaster car that had just plunged over the edge, into the abyss. There was roaring in his ears and he felt himself begin to sweat. What was happening to him?

He picked up his black XeroxWorld '92 mug with shaking hands and looked into it wondering if the coffee had been made too strong that morning. He shouldn't have had that double latté on top of it. Looking around the conference room, everything looked strange and foreign and what he saw made him shudder. Run, run, get away, it's not worth it, came a voice from inside. Ted looked at the door, planning his escape. His muscles tensed.

Then, just as quickly as it came, the feeling passed. Everything returned to normal and once again he was Ted Heath, Director of Marketing, sitting and waiting his boss to arrive. He shook his head, smiled to himself. He resolved to switch to decaf once XOS 4.0 shipped.

"Ted," Bob said. "You alright?"

"Yeah, yeah," Ted responded and attempted a smile that he realized from Bob's reaction was as grotesque as it felt. "Just a passing thing. I think someone made the coffee too strong this morning."

"Yeah, I've been meaning to ask Mary about that," Bob nodded, and then looked away, perhaps infected by the same anxiety that had gripped Ted the moment before.

A breeze rustled through the conference room, stirring the printed emails and notebooks on the table. Before Ted could think in detail about how a breeze could penetrate the four doorways that separated the conference room from the outside world, a tall, impressive figure dressed in black strode into the conference room and gazed imperiously at the people assembled there.

Reflexively, Ted sat up at attention. After a moment's thought, though, he realized that the figure was not anyone he knew at XCS, and on top of that, had certainly never been employed there. He was tall, almost too tall, wearing black trousers and a black shirt, of a fabric that Ted could not identify, perhaps because it was of such a blackness so deep it seemed to suck the very light of the room into it. Perched jauntily on his head was a fine cloth beret, and most absurdly of all, he carried in his left hand a black antique cane with a silver dog's head on it.

At first the visitor seemed stern, perhaps disapproving, but then he broke into a charming smile and tapped the carpeted floor with his cane, making a much louder sound than it should have.

"Good morning. I am Dr. Woland. The Consultant."

"Ah," Ted found himself saying, but no words followed this initial sound and it came out seeming horribly rude.

Beverly cut in smoothly, at the same time casting a sharp, questioning glance at Ted. "Good morning. On behalf of the team, welcome." After just the slightest pause, she continued. "We received the email from John but... he didn't say anything... about your role..." Beverly kept pausing, giving the Consultant a chance to step in and explain his presence, but he said nothing, just stood in front of them, resting his hands on the dog's head of his cane.

After her last pause, Beverly gave up and fell silent. The Consultant, if indeed that was what he was, merely took one of the chairs with an elegant motion, pulled it out, sat, crossed his long legs and lay his cane carefully against the edge of the beige table.

Bob cleared his throat. Beverly closed the lid of her Xerox Flare 250 with a metallic click. The marketing temp awoke with a start, as if from a bad dream. He looked around wildly as if he had never seen any of them before and had forgotten even who he was.

"I'm happy to see that you're all here," the Consultant said after this bizarrely long pause. "It makes it all so much more convenient. I assume you all received Mr. Faust's email."

"Uh, of course, I just said that," Beverly said. "So you're a consultant."

"Yes. Perhaps I should explain in further detail. For reasons that I am unable to go into right now, Mr. Faust has transferred authority over the XOS 4.0 roll-out to me–"

With this, a tremendous hubbub erupted in the room. Abraham blinked furiously as Bob gaped in disbelief. Beverly uttered a single, anguished, "What?"

"But that's ridiculous, John would never do that." Ted said, realizing as did that it was obvious, the Consultant was an impostor; he was mentally disturbed; he had somehow stolen a badge; it was a practical joke by John to release tension; there had to some kind of reasonable explanation.

The Consultant held up his hand and somehow all the commotion stopped. "Nevertheless. He has." The Consultant took a gold pocket watch out and flipped the cover open foppishly. "I believe he has a scheduled a video-conference for right now. Ted, if you would."

Without thinking, and barely conscious of his body's motions as if he were possessed, Ted turned and activated the LCD panel on the wall to his side. A menu appeared in black letters on light grey background.

"Relay channel C, I believe," the Consultant said.

Ted touched the words on the screen. Instantly–far too fast, really, with none of the usual delay in establishing the video stream–the harried face of John Faust filled the screen. For a second he looked disoriented, then glanced to his left. His face broke out in a tired smile.

"Ah, Ted, Bev, Bob. I see you've met Dr. Woland."

"Yes," Beverly said indignantly, "And he says you've handed the rollout off to him, John, what–"

John held up his hand and flashed a reassuring smile.

"Don't worry, Bev. You'll be in excellent hands. Dr. Woland's the best in the world at his business. I don't believe he has any competitors."

"No, not for many years," Dr. Woland said matter-of-factly.

"What does he do?" Beverly asked.

John didn't seem to hear her question and instead smiled, this time in his "let's wrap up the meeting" mode. "Unfortunately, I have business far away."

"Very far away, indeed," said Dr. Woland with a cat-like smile of pleasure. "Almost nowhere that's farther," he added, mostly to himself.

"Good luck," John said, "I'll be in touch,"

The screen returned to light grey. Beverly slumped and looked defeated. Bob shrugged. The marketing temp took a sip of water and continued taking notes on his pad of paper.

"Not that that's settled," the Consultant said, "Shall we get started?"

Okay, now that you've read it, you may have some questions. First off, I titled the work "Mrs. Faust" because the main character was John Faust wife, but she doesn't appear in first chapter, as you can see. I vaguely recall writing a scene with her at home, bored out of her mind and gossiping with a neighbor, but it turns out that I only write a description of it, an example of the danger of making notes instead of actually writing.

Also, if the setting of the story seems a bit strange (I don't remember Xerox making groupware software—and how is Microsoft such a small company) that's because I set Mrs. Faust *in an alternate reality in which Xerox capitalized on the innovations from their PARC research facility, and ended up being the dominant company in computers and software.*

The previous selection was written at time when the tech industry was waiting for the release of "Chicago" aka Windows 4.0, which had been in development for more than three years. That inspired me to include a similar event in my parallel universe. Windows 4.0, renamed 95, finally came out in August 1995, and led to a decade of dominance by Microsoft of the desktop computing space.

I don't know why that parallel tech reality was relevant to a reworking of the Faust myth. Maybe I was just subconsciously bored with my Faust/Master & Margarita obsession and looking for a way to make it more fun for me. I had learned something about the history of the software business from working with my father on the Apple v. Microsoft case, so it was fun to be able to use what I head learned in my fiction. Parallel universes are a popular sub-genre of fiction, but they usually depict alternate realities where the south won the civil war or the Nazis conquered Great Britain, not ones in which the history of technology takes a different course.

One more note before we move on: I gave one of the characters the last name of Garfunkel as a tribute to an odd bit of personal trivia. During my first temp assignment in fall 1991, I worked with a technical writer with that name, who was indeed the brother of Paul Simon's former musical partner. He was quite tall, but lacked the characteristic cloud of frizzy hair.

Later in 1995, I started another Tim novel, one that was not set in Santa Zita during college (look at me, branching out!), but instead based on my life in 1995–living in San Francisco and temping, but dreaming of road trips, escape from the quotidian, and some greater destiny.

The title is in quotes because this was a time when, inspired by my time in the software industry, I had started giving codenames to future projects. When I first conceived of the Santa Zita Stories *project, I gave each one a single word nickname.* Stealing Money, *for example, was "Capone" and* Helen of Santa Zita *got the somewhat misogynistic codename "Scarlet," a reference to both the Nathaniel Hawthorne novel and the Whore of Babylon. It's a practice I still adhere to, given that the final volume of the Santa Zita novels is currently codenamed "Margarita."*

Continuing my quixotic (see what I did there?) practice of making every one of my novels a parallel with a major work of western literature, "Conquistador" was my attempt to rewrite

Cervantes's Don Quixote as a story of a temp worker roaming the country and getting into various amusing, picaresque adventures.

I should note that the fact that this piece has footnotes but none of the others do is not a bug. They were a feature of the original composition, a meta-fictional gambit I thought might be amusing. When I prepared this piece for inclusion in ISoNIA, I thought about removing them, but since they provide some useful information of that time and place, and are true to what I thought was cool and funny at the time, I decided to leave them in.

"Conquistador"

Chapter the First, in which Timothy becomes dissatisfied with Temping, and thinks of leaving San Francisco.

All the jobs for next week were data entry.

On Friday evening Timothy Page[1] returned from his job downtown for the last time, his temporary assignment at the Fidelity One Investments marketing department having ended that day. It had lasted three months, two more than he expected, and one more than he really wanted.

Now Tim stood over the phone, one hand holding the receiver to his ear, the other over his chest like he was saying the pledge of allegiance. As he listened to the voicemail messages from the three agencies he was registered with, he felt the mad beat of his heart. He had drunk too much coffee that day. Two cups in the morning, a latté after lunch. He had gotten so bored with his job that the only way he could make

---

[1] A character by this name was also used in Hall's earlier novel, *The Deep & Savage Way*. However, there are inconsistencies between the two, as yet unexplained. Thus, *Conquistador* can not really be considered a sequel proper.

himself go back after lunch was to bribe himself with a double latté from Spinelli's[2].

Tim towered over the phone on its low table, reading his apartment's phone list while he listened to the friendly and efficient voices for temp agency's assignment coordinator; they were always women, even in San Francisco.

First, Margery from ProTemps. Data entry, nine dollars an hour. Tim dismissed it out of hand, the rate of pay was far too low to interest him, now that he was earning fifteen, sixteen sometimes even eighteen, at Costiloe & Davis Management Consultancy.

The next message was from Carrie at MacTemps[3]. "Tim, I have a something that starts Monday, it's not too exciting, but it is at Fidelity One."

"Sounds cool," he said, as if Carrie had been in the same room as him. She didn't hear him, of course, but continued speaking in a flattering voice. "It's at customer service; you know, where you worked before. They asked for you back specifically; you know, because of all the good work you did there last time."

Tim had worked there before, a pleasant backwater in the archipelago of buildings housing Fidelity One, clustered around Market Street in downtown San Francisco. It was the department the company placed people too incompetent to work in the parts of the business that actually made money, but too nice to fire. The sort of friendly, mediocre people who had majored in Communications and gotten a B average at UC San Diego or UC Santa Barbara. They had remembered him,

---

[2] A chain of coffee shops located in the San Francisco Bay Area region. It was purchased in 1996 by Tully's, a much larger, and decidedly inferior, chain based in Seattle.

[3] MacTemps was an example of a temp agency; i.e., a company that places workers in temporary positions. In exchange for finding them work, they took a hefty cut of the hourly rate the businesses paid for the temps' time.

even though he had only worked there for a week. Still, he had no desire to return.

He listened to the third message. Another data entry job, at the San Francisco AIDS Foundation. "They asked for you back by name," Tricia's voice said through the phone, with a mixture of praise and expectation in her voice.

Once again, Tim felt the sting of the temp's sense of obligation. To be asked back by name was the ultimate compliment. According to Tim's temp code of honor, when you were asked back, you always went. The temp agency had to know that you were an asset, a person that people remembered with pleasure–the kind that didn't say no.

But this time, it wasn't enough. Spending a week in the Foundation's grey, brown and light green office, working through never-ending stacks of torn-off cardboard BRCs[4] held together by brittle rubber-bands that broke at the slightest provocation, seemed now to be an intolerable prospect to Tim.

The final job, offered by a lower-grade agency that Tim had only registered with as a backup to Pro and MacTemps, offered him a data entry job in the "orders processing department" at Liberty Shipping, a name which made Tim imagine dusty 286 PCs[5] running DOS and hooked into a cryptic order entry database where you had to type ctrl-\-m before every command, and even a single typo could result in the loss of several minutes work, with the end result that it would have been just as efficient to do the whole thing in

---

[4] Business Reply Cards. In the pre-Internet era, they were small rectangular pieces of cardboard that people filled out and mailed to businesses in order to get more information. Since they were handwritten, it usually required a live person to enter the data into the computer.

[5] The x86 series of Intel microchips powered IBM-standard Windows PCs during the late 80s and 90s. By 1995 the 486 was the current standard, so a 286 was at least two generations behind, thus considered to be positively antiquated.

hand-written ledgers, or by knotting pieces of string like the Incas.

What would be even worse were the people who worked there. They would barely qualified as San Franciscans; instead living in places like Brisbane, Burlingame, or Milbrae. They would be older and filled with a growing quiet desperation, aware on some instinctive, biological level that their employer's business was becoming more and more irrelevant to the economy of the Bay Area, as the information lords in the city and Silicon Valley created the future, in which the United States no longer dealt in the crass business of actually making or moving anything physical and tangible (leaving that to the emerging economies of the Far East and Latin America) but instead just created and manipulated information. The herd they moved with was doomed, and they knew it. Every year they earned less, had their hours and benefits cut, were laid off and replaced by temps like Tim.

They had evolved to survive in a doomed ecosystem, dependent on waterholes that were becoming smaller and smaller every year. At the same time, the number of leaner and faster predators harassing them increased. They were the zebra who zigged when the rest of the herd zagged and got taken by the cheetah lying in wait. Knocked down, claws raking across her flank, intestines spilling out. The rest of the herd moved on, knowing they were temporarily safe.

Though Tim acknowledged the inevitability of history, he hated being part of the process; of coming into a business and knowing that he was doing twice as much work for half the cost, and that the other employees there knew it, and also realized the company cared nothing for them. Indeed, it was only organizational inertia and possible public relations problems that kept them from laying everybody and replacing them with a small coterie of highly-paid programmers and an army of Tims, people who were young and would work for eight dollars an hour and no benefits because they could. The thirty-five year old women who had to have health insurance because she had kids was cast aside.

As Tim thought about that, he suddenly felt distanced from the whole phenomenon, like he was watching a nature documentary as the narrator remorselessly, and yet reassuringly, described how the cheetah did the antelopes a favor by culling the herd of the old and the weak. Was that all it ever amounted to? Were he and other temps like him lean, hungry predators, more efficient and adaptable and thus more worthy to survive? There had to be more meaning in life than that. It sickened Tim, that by doing his job well, the only way he knew how, the only way that would make him happy, he would be thoughtlessly destroying other people's lives.

In any case, he didn't want the job.

Once Tim finished listening to his messages, he thought about his temp's code of honor. He had been temping for so long, he had evolved a system of values that made him feel better about such things. Since many companies hired by "auditioning" potential employees by hiring them as temps first, workplaces frequently viewed every temp who came along as a potential employee. That meant the confident employees treated you nicely, as a potential future ally in office politics, while the marginal employees saw you as a threat. Either could lead to trouble.

When Tim first arrived at a new assignment, he always made it completely clear that he was only passing through, that he had no intention of settling down or taking someone's job. He declined to participate in any office social function, offering as an excuse the fact that he was paid by the hour, so it would be unfair to spend it on non-productive activities.

Tim had once typed the rules down into his PowerBook. They went as follows:

i) never do anything menial, avoid aggressive servility
ii) remain faithful to yourself, your job at hand and your code,
not your agency or company you're working at
iii) never attempt to take anyone's permanent job
iv) never ask to leave an assignment before it's done
v) never become personally involved with a regular employee
vi) always go back if you're asked

Tim had thought about publishing them, in a guide to temping or something. If the economy kept going the way it had been, people might start to spend their whole lives temping and there would have to be new social codes and mores to guide them, to stave off anarchy, the Darwinian jungle that Tim saw lurking everywhere in civilization.

So far he had only gone so far as to put it into PageMaker, formatted with some fancy Adobe PostScript fonts he had copied from work, a violation of his ethical code, perhaps, but a harmless one. He had printed out a copy for Patty, but she hadn't understood it. She didn't worry about stuff like that. She worked, came home, ate food, and did something fun. If she was a pawn in a war between culture and the abyss, she didn't notice or care. Tim envied that ability, but he couldn't live that way.

Despite the requirements of the code, Tim decided he would reject all of the assignments on offer. He couldn't quite bring himself to do it immediately, so he saved the messages on the voicemail by repeatedly pressing "2." He crossed the dining room and went to the window.

Overhead, the fog blew in from the ocean, looking like a speeded-up film of clouds in the desert. Dreams of flight filled his mind. For two years he had lived in San Francisco. He temped, he rented month-to-month, he wasn't married, had no children, no pets; he didn't even own a houseplant. Nothing chained him, the way they chained the people who had permanent jobs at the companies he temped at–yet he stayed.

In spite of his pretensions, Tim was really no different than people who had regular jobs, except that they had at least had something to show for their commitments–a sense of security, of nurturing and establishing a life. He hadn't grown, like a tree planted in the soil, and he hadn't flourished from roaming free as a mountain lion would. What exactly was he? Mold? No, more like an animal that didn't move around very much but had no actual nest. Like a big green tree-snake, or something.

He could leave at any time, he knew. This idea has surfaced in his mind with more and more frequency since the previous winter. He had almost five thousand dollars saved, he had a (somewhat)-functioning car. At any moment, he could disappear into the highways and byways of the United States, settle in any town, any state, any region, in places he knew only from endless hours of data entry; Spokane, WA; Bismarck, ND, Huntsville, AL; Flagstaff, AZ; Albuquerque, NM; Tallahassee, FL; cities that in their ordinariness had a certain allure.

The idea of leaving everything behind and hitting the highway reminded him of books and movies, like *On the Road*, and *Wild At Heart*, or *The Grapes of Wrath*[6] when people had to move or die. There were certain times in history that were like that. What if this were one of them, and no one realized it? Maybe the little signs, the crime, the increased tension, the guns and gangs, the drive-by shootings, were signals that everyone tried to ignore, but shouldn't. Tim imagined people in linen suits and flowery dresses, sitting in a seaside hotel in Brazil and sipping espresso under a under a green and yellow

---

[6] All three of the works mentioned are famous road books or movies. For a discussion of the Mosaic connections between them, seem John Hurle's essay "The Moses Trip".

parasol. It was spring 1939 and they had left Europe a year before. They read in the papers about the invasion of Poland and thanked God that they had read the signs right and gotten out just in time.

Tim remembered the riots in 1992[7], when they had sat in the living room with the windows open and heard the shouts of the mob as people marched downtown. On the radio they listened to the hysterical voices of helicopter pilots describing the burning of South Central LA. Ever since those terrifying six days there had been that dread lurking, the fear that everything could fall apart again. The sinking feeling in his stomach as he thought there might not be a future, or a future any one would want to live in, the same fear he'd had as a kid when he thought about nuclear war.

Tim longed to go out of time, to change his life so drastically and so suddenly, he could find out if the rest of the world existed; or if it were all some kind of alien experiment, that he lived in an artificial human habitat All of the talk about "North Dakota," "Oklahoma," and "Georgia" was just a carefully constructed fiction, a part of the experiment. To pull it off, all the aliens would need to actually build were the Bay Area, Boston, Paris, and the other places he had traveled.

Tim decided it was time for him to fly. He wished he had been smoking while looking out the window, so could have stubbed out his cigarette and tossed the butt out the window to show his resolve. Instead, he shut the window and reached for the phone to call Patty.

---

[7] The author is almost certainly referring to the Rodney King Riots of April 29-May 4 1992, when residents of Los Angeles erupted in fury after the policemen accused of beating the eponymous man were acquitted of all crimes by an all-white jury.

Chapter the Second, in which Timothy tells Patty of his Plan.

"I'm thinking of disappearing," Tim blurted out later that night after several beers.

Patty looked at him with narrowed brown eyes as Tim took a swig of oatmeal stout. Whenever he went out for a night of drinking, Tim always switched to stouts after the first few beers, because they were lower in alcohol and higher in food-value–important for a person with a high metabolic rate.

"Where to?" she asked. "And why?"

"Where? Anywhere. Why? Because I can. I think it's what I need to do."

"But–"

"I was thinking today," Tim cut her off, speaking breathlessly, as he looked at the fog racing overhead. "I have all this freedom. but I don't use it. I have a car, money, no commitments. I should be..." Tim waved his arms. "Doing something."

Patty looked down into her beer that had been almost empty for an hour.

"But then I decided not to."

"What changed your mind?"

"What would I do, really? I'd go for about two weeks, have an okay time, and then get lonely. Traveling by yourself really sucks. I mean, for someone like me. I did it once in Europe. The only way this trip could work is if after a few days of going by myself I gradually met a bunch of zany-yet-cool companions who would perfectly mesh with my personality and formed a perfect unit. Then we'd be off to see the wizard. But that would never happen."

Patty focused her eyes intently on Tim for a second, opened her mouth to say something, but then stopped.

"What?" Tim asked.

"Well..." She smiled suddenly, lighting up her face and making her seem much prettier for a moment. "Then take me with you. I'd go."

"You would?" Tim took a tremendous gulp of stout and returned Patty's intense gaze searchingly.

"Yes."

"But you have a real job."

"I can quit. I'm not going anywhere at Fidelity. My boss doesn't like me that much, but I'm too good at my job to fire. If I stay there I'll just end up doing the same thing forever."

"Wow. I never..." Tim felt foolish. In retrospect, it felt like he had told Patty he didn't like traveling alone in order to get exactly this result. Like he was desperate, but in fact he had never entertained the possibility. Why, he wasn't sure.

"Never what?"

"Imagined you would be interested, in this kind of thing."

"Then let's go. Let's go tomorrow."

"Well, not tomorrow."

"Then the day after. Come on, Tim. Let's have an adventure." Patty smiled, and after a second, Tim smiled back and brushed the hair off his forehead.

Patty was Tim's one close friend in San Francisco who wasn't from Santa Zita. She was also the only friend he had ever made while temping. Tim's temping code required that he keep to himself, never getting emotionally or socially entangled with his co-workers no matter how long he worked at an assignment. Usually they didn't try. Nobody really knew how long you would be there, and beyond a limited attempt to make you feel welcome and part of the team (inviting you to small office functions and offering you birthday cake, for example, which they often did because the older women in the office seemed to think he was dangerously underweight) they didn't concern themselves with you.

Patty had been different. She had sought Tim out. After only two weeks in the Fidelity One marketing department, she had asked Tim out to lunch cold. Tim had been taken so off-guard, that he had no time to think of any of his usual excuses for missing office functions. They had fun, and Tim found he enjoyed talking to someone for whom all of his jokes and stories were new.

After further discussion, the plan they came up with was this: to drive Tim's car around the nation, roaming from place to place. Every so often, if they needed money, they would settle down for just a month or two and temp. There were potential difficulties, like the fact they might have to keep re-registering, but if they were both registered with a national agency like Kelly, Tim thought it might not be so hard, they could just have their file transferred from city to city.

Later that night, Patty wrote in her diary:

May 22, 1993

Last night Tim suddenly had this weird idea. He wants to drive across the county and live in different towns, temping to make ends meet, just because he wants "to really see America."

I don't know why, but I told him I wanted to come. I think I managed to surprise him. Yay! (I hardly ever do.) I'm still not sure why I said it, though. I mean, I really have a life here in SF, unlike Tim—I've got a job and all my friends are here.

It would be weird not to have Tim around, though. I'm sort of used to talking to him, now, and he's a good listener, most of the time, when he remembers not to pass judgment on everything.

It's just the same old problem that I keep telling you about, diary. He's just so attractive in this goofy way. Everything he does he does because it just occurred to him that moment. Either that or he has so some weird plan that only he would think of, and once he thinks of it he has to do it. It becomes this, like, fixation. Like that time he decided he was going to listen to every single CD he owns, in the order he acquired them, and he did. It took him a month, and he refused to listen to any other music until he did. It was sort of fun, actually, when I was hanging out with him I heard a lot of albums I hadn't listened to in a long time.

This thing about driving around the country—lots of people would have that idea and never actually do it, but Tim will. I've never seen someone who lives so much on the surface of their skin. When he has one of his weird ideas and gets all enthusiastic about it, I can't help but get drawn in.

It's just that, can I really imagine spending six months, or a year (?!?! Really?!), with just him. Talk about commitment! I must be crazy.

Chapter the Third, in which Tim experiences Doubt.

On Saturday night, Tim's friend Sophie was having a party at her new apartment in Cole Valley. That afternoon was a typical San Francisco spring day, alternating between bright sun and grey fog, with a cold breeze blowing down the hill from Upper Haight (once called the Haight-Ashbury) down into Lower. It was a blank, blah sort of day, the kind that drove Tim crazy, reminding him of the bad times in his life.

Tim's housemates all disappeared early–Jake and Anna went off biking in Marin while Todd was spending the day in Alta Lara, visiting his parents. Tim drank too much grainy coffee from his demitasse coffee-maker, and spent a few hours goofing around on his Powerbook with FileMaker Pro until he realized it was already two o'clock and that he needed to motivate if he was going to make anything of that day.

Tim decided to take his Powerbook 160 to a nearby cafe and work on his "novel". This project, which he had been working on and off since he left UCSZ, was his primary hope for a better life. Without it, he thought, he was really no different from thousands of other suburban kids who had gone to state universities, moved to the city, and started temping at office jobs. The novel was what made him unique, the one inalienable expression of his own individuality that was permanent and would last beyond his death.

Unfortunately, his novel was also a complete mess. It consisted of a variety of different MacWrite and Microsoft Word files (the novel had spanned several different generations of Macintosh, from the Mac Plus to the Powerbook) all begun and abandoned at different times. Most of the fragments he had actually written were based on Tim's experiences in college, as the main character, Steven, had gradually become exposed to drugs, alcohol and vice (in the great *bildungsroman* tradition) on his way to discovering his true calling, to become an artist. Along with that were a healthy dose of flashbacks to the character's growing up in thinly fictionalized version of Alta Lara named Palo Alto, explaining how Steven had become who he was, particularly his distant and hopeless love for Jessica.

Tim talked about his novel a lot, but he had not actually shown it to anyone except Patty. She had read the first twenty pages (at a time the previous fall when Tim had completely rethought the project and written a whole new start from scratch). Thought Tim had told her several times it was just fiction, she asked him after she finished the first five pages "who's Jessica?" knowing that she was a real person. That was how Tim had ended up telling her about Melissa. After that, Tim had never shown her any more of it, or even asked her what she thought of its merits as a work of art.

Tim's long-term goal now was to somehow piece together all of the disparate fragments and chapters, the flashbacks, the college scenes, as well as the "Stephanie tragedy" about beautiful Stephanie's tragic love for Andrew, who is blind to anyone but the memory of Jessica (not based on Tim's life) and most importantly the ending. He wanted the novel to end happily, in defiance of all stereotypes. Against all odds, years later, Andrew and Jessica meet again and she falls in love with him, when Andrew goes to the city she lives in and assumes a new identity, successful writer Brad Stevenson, interpolating himself into her milieu. After a month of going out together, one night in bed Andrew becomes overcome with guilt and wakes Jessica up, to tell that he's not Brad Stevenson but Andrew High. "Oh," Jessica says after a moment, "I knew that all along, but so what. I still love you." Then they proceed to have amazing sex. Tim knew that would be the ending. How could you top that?

The problem was getting there.

At the café, Tim got lucky and scored one of the cool seats, little tables tucked into a nook between the door and the wall, looking out on the sidewalk. After reading the *Guardian* all the way through, he sat and watched the alternations outside between bright sunlight, which made the street seem warm, inviting and full of promise, and grey, which made everything seem washed out, pointless—the fog seeming to saturate his brain and prevent any useful activity.

Scattered in front of him were pages of his novel, printed in different paper and printers—in the folder where Tim kept the edited pages of his novel one could trace the history and development of computer printers, from dot-matrix, to inkjet, to higher and higher resolution laser, culminating in the 600 dpi printouts he had made while he was working at Fidelity One, a rare violation of his code of honor, but which he thought was allowable, given the times he had worked a little bit later than the time he had put down on his timecard, since he always rounded down instead of up.

From the bottom of the folder Tim took one of the oldest paper-clipped bunches, printed on an original Apple ImageWriter, and looked closely at the little dark grey dots, enjoying the look of the New York twelve point font. There was something intrinsically cool about it; once futuristic but now retro, like BART train cars or Buck Rogers' nacelled spaceship, and in some ways Tim wished he had never given up his old Mac Plus and its attendant ImageWriter, the writing system he had used his entire time at college. He reread the pages he had extracted and sighed. He wished he had just written the entire thing, because there were flashback scenes to Steven and Jessica's first encounters he had just summarized that he wasn't sure he could do justice to, the details of early 80s Alta Lara were slipping away from him.

The reason Tim had to take the entire folder around with him when he worked on his novel was that all of his printouts had important corrections on them, and sometimes substantial additions in pencil which he could hardly read, that he needed to enter into the computer files, but never had.

Another low cloud passed overhead and once again the street was cast in gloom. Tim looked and saw a homeless man shuffle down the street, followed by two gay men walking their small brown dog. A breeze shivered through the trees and Tim saw the two men put their hands in their pocket. Suddenly the prospect of a drive across the country seemed an impossible prospect, an insane scheme doomed to failure. He tried to imagine he and Patty spending six months with just each other and his mind drew a blank. He just couldn't see it. Their friendship was fine the way it was but they would drive each other crazy in such close quarters. She didn't inspire him enough; he needed someone like Melissa or Helen, or Sophie at least, to accompany him on adventure like this. Patty just didn't move him in the same way. And his car, ROSE83, she would never make it even halfway across the country. He only had $5000 saved up, which seemed like a lot until you considered that he would have to pay for everything, and that they would be staying in motels a lot, not to mention the cost of gas. How long would it last?

Maybe he should just take a short trip later in the summer. He could go visit his friend Helen, who had settled in Seattle. He had never been up there, and always wanted to, it was becoming so trendy and seemed to be sort of a center of 90s culture in a way, what with Nirvana, Starbucks, and Microsoft all being up there.

Closing the cover of his Powerbook with a satisfying click, Tim decided to tell Patty that night at Sophie's party that he had decided not to go.

Ed. Note: I had then planned a scene where Tim expressed his doubts to Patty at Sophie's party, but she stiffened his resolve. I never got around to it, so you will just have to pretend you read it.

Chapter the Fourth, in which Tim goes to Jake for Guidance and Benediction for the Journey ahead.

Jake was one of Tim's closest friends–they had met their freshman year at the University of California, Santa Zita and been friends for all four years of school. The fall after their graduation, they had found an apartment together in San Francisco.

When it became known to Tim that he had to leave on his journey, Jake was the first person he had to tell. Not only because he was Tim's closest male friend, but because he was also the tacitly acknowledged leader of their household, the one who handled all of their contact with the landlord, it was Tim's formal duty to give notice that he would be leaving the apartment.

Tim accomplished this duty over a pint of Red Tail Ale[8] at the Toronado[9], filling Jake in on the plan he had made with Patty.

"Well..." Jake said, shaking his head. "Wow."

"Yeah, I know. Kind of a surprise. Sorry."

"No, no. I mean, I'm happy for you. That sounds awesome. How much money do you have saved?"

"Almost five thousand."

Jake shook his head, this time with a touch of reverence. "Man. I had no idea it was that much."

Tim shrugged, smiled shyly. "Temping pays pretty well, if you know PowerPoint."

"And you're just going to... leave."

"Day after tomorrow."

"Rolling down the open road..." Something occurred to Jake. "You're taking your car? The blue one?"

"Yeah," Tim said. "She can handle it. I think."

"Hmh. She does kind of vibrate."

"Oh, that's not serious. I mean, I've had her looked at it, and it's just an idiosyncrasy of the car, not a problem. One of those weird things that's bothersome but not really worth fixing."

---

[8] A brand of micro-brewed ale made by the Mendocino Brewing Company.

[9] A bar located in San Francisco's Lower Haight district, also mentioned in two other contemporary novels, Douglas Coupland's *Microserfs* and *A Heartbreaking Work of Staggering Genius* by Dave Eggers.

"If you say so."

"Anyway," Tim said. "I know this kind of sucks for you, but... it's something I have to do. I've been here for two years, I need something new."

"I hear you," Jake said. "I totally think it's cool. I just wish I could go."

"You could."

"Haven't saved enough money, so I can't quit my job. Plus there's Anna. It's something I think about a lot. Just hopping on a motorcycle and escaping."

"It's tempting. It's tempted me. Except for the motorcycle part."

"Now," Jake said, and a slight smile curled his lips. "You're going with Patty...?"

"Yeah, I told her about it and she said she wanted to go with me. I'm kind of blown away, it's a bigger deal for her. She's actually going to quit her job."

"She likes you."

"I know. I wished I liked her. I mean, well, you know what I mean."

"You never know what can happen when you travel."

Jake and Tim gave each other serious nods. "Well, it won't happen with us," Tim said. "I've got a sense of honor about this kind of thing."

"We'll see. Send us a postcard, if you guys do get together," Jake said, and leered again. "

Okay," said Tim, rolling his eyes.

After a pause, in which they both surveyed the bar, Jake turned his attention back to Tim. "Maybe you should wait, Jake said. Until August. Anna and I are planning to go out to the mountains for a while. You and Patty could come."

"Yeah," Tim said. "That's a thought."

"If we all drove together, we could split gas."

"It's kind of a lot of people, though, in one car."

"Uh huh. But, dude, are you really ready to leave? So suddenly?"

"Sure. What's keeping me here?"

"Well, I don't know," Jake said, and looked down.

"I'm sorry. I didn't mean it that way. Of course I'll miss you, and Anna, and Sophie and everyone. But it's time to leave. I can feel it. Remember at Sophie's place, in Galena?"

"Remember what?"

"When we went there a month ago, and we saw the geese flying south for the summer. When I saw them, I suddenly felt this intense need to go with them, this longing that swelled in my breast. It was like something in a German poem."

"Wow. Well, if it's like that, if it's in your heart, then you gotta do it."

"So I have your blessing?" Tim held out his hand, fingers spread apart and upside-down.

"Yeah, of course. Dude, you're going to have an amazing time."

"Cheers to that." Tim raised his pint glass. Jake lifted his and they toasted over the table.

"Cheers," Jake said. "And good luck."

Chapter the Fifth, in which Tim and Patty cross the Great Nevada Desert.

Appalling vistas of nothingness passed by them on either side. Patty slumped next to him, her head resting awkwardly in such a way that the rectangular patch of sunlight coming through the window missed her eyes.

Tim gently eased ROSE83 past seventy–but before we proceed further, something should be said about Tim's car: a blue four-door sedan, license plate ROSE83. Roses were Tim's mother's favorite kind of flower, and the car had been purchased in 1983, which explained the vanity plate. Not very sleek, dented in two places, and lacking three of her four hubcaps, she made up for these deficiencies with a certain tenacious reliability. No matter how much Tim neglected her; and he was as incompetent with automobiles as he was skilled with computers; how many times he forgot to check the oil, avoid maintenance, add water, she kept running. She was a tribute to a certain era of Japanese engineering, a triumph of their civilization like the Romans' aqueducts, the Mayans' pyramids and the Americans' skyscrapers—the apex of their ability to make basic, reliable cars before they succumbed to imperial over-reach and decadence, their auto-makers spinning off luxury divisions with fake, Latinate sounding names; the inevitable decay, just as the Romans had turned their engineering ability from building roads and aqueducts to constructing coliseums where they watched lions eating Christians; sating the bloodlust of the masses with gladiatorial games and slaughter.

Now that you have all that in mind, let us return to Tim gently easing ROSE83 past seventy. He wanted to see just how fast she could go on a straight-away. Her engine whined, but not too bad. At seventy-five, however, the whine increased to such a degree that Tim thought she might be actually be in pain. He took pity and brought her back down, trying to get the speedometer needle to rest as precisely between seventy and seventy-five as he could.

This activity amused him for another ten minutes, at which point he had to go around a large camper going only fifty-five. Doing so reminded Tim how his driving speed fit awkwardly between the slow drivers, the campers, trucks and decrepit cars who could only go between fifty and sixty, and everyone else on the road, who all went eighty or faster, going as fast as possible if only as an antidote to insanity. Then there was Tim, constantly having to pass the really slow people but unwilling to go as fast as the prevailing traffic in the fast lane. Thus, he spent much of his time switching lanes, which at least gave him something to do.

Once Tim was well past the latest clump of campers and semi-trailers and back in the slow lane, he looked around the landscape, amazed by the endless variety of nothing on both sides. It was as if God Himself could get bored, have an off day creating the world, one in which He just couldn't get inspired and think of anything really cool to make; instead He just kind of phoned it in. Perhaps He had made Nevada just as an interim placeholder, a geographical *lorem ipsum*, until He could come back and do something really worthwhile with it, and then forgotten, distracted by the Devil's rebellion, the Adam and Eve fiasco, Cain and Abel, and then the Flood, the Exodus, the Passion and everything since then, a lower-priority task forever remaining near the bottom of God's to-do list.

However, the part of Tim's brain educated at UCSZ reminded him, this was a western-European imperialist patriarchal way of looking at it. In fact, all landscapes were equally valid. There had been Indians living here; to them; it must have been as beautiful, comfortable, and interesting as Alta Lara or Santa Zita was to him. Or did they get tired of it, too? They were nomadic, so maybe they too tired of endless hills with clumps of brown-green plants, and they moved on, went west to the Sierras. Would they think of that as a vacation? To nomads, a vacation would be a meaningless concept, since they were always in motion; it was the very definition of their way of life. Maybe to them a vacation was staying in one place for a while, remaining there even when they were supposed to be moving on.

Patty stirred. The sun had landed on her face again. She blinked furiously, sat up and looked around with puffy, recessed eyes.

"Where are we?" she said in a scratchy voice.

"The same place we were two hours ago, judging by the landscape."

"No," she said, irritably, "really, where?"

Tim shrugged. "Still between Winnemucca and Elko."

"Oh, God." Patty took a drink of warm orange-flavored Calistoga.

"Did you sleep?"

"Yeah, and now I have a headache."

"Awww." Tim touched her sympathetically on the shoulder.

Squinting, Patty looked down the Interstate, which now curved slightly around a mountain shoulder. Ahead of them loomed a line of semis.

"More trucks," Tim said. "A convoy," he said, relishing the associations, thinking of CB radios and men with bushy mustaches, driving their semis side by side and staring down a phalanx of state troopers.

"Do you want me to do some driving?" Patty asked.

"No, I'm fine. Actually, I'm enjoying it, in a really strange way. The sensation of seeing an endless variety of nothing different for hours and hours is quite meditative."

Patty didn't seem to share his opinion. "I'm going to try to sleep some more." She contorted her head in a new position so the sun wouldn't be on her face, and closed her eyes.

An hour later, the Nevada desert's seemingly infinite supply of yellow hills had ceased to amuse Tim in any way. He found himself calculating to two decimal points the exact amount of time until they reached Elko. Glancing at the landscape no longer made him think about anything other than the fact that he was tired of it, more tired of it than seemed humanly possible. He was thirsty, too, and the warm bottled water he was drinking provided no relief. He longed for a cold soda, or a frothy pint of something hoppy–anything cool and soothing.

Another line of trucks appeared in the distance as Tim's car reached the top of a small rise. Tim checked the fast lane in his rearviewmirror[10] and saw a large black pickup truck coming from a few hundred yards behind them. Looking ahead, Tim realized that the semis were moving even slower than they usually did, perhaps because the road was starting to incline upwards again.

Tim flipped on his turn signal and moved into the fast lane, in the same motion whipping his head around to make sure the way was still unobstructed, just out of habit. The black pickup was right behind him, looming over the road with a shiny chrome grille that reflected the sun with a blinding flash, a behemoth now slowing but appearing angry, as if it wanted to swallow the hapless Japanese car that possessed the gall to get in its way.

Tim pressed down the accelerator. "Come on, ROSE83," he exhorted his car.

Looking up at the rearviewmirror, Tim could feel the black pickup's contempt of his small blue car and its desire to speed faster. He tried to push ROSE83 up to 80, made even more difficult that the road was becoming steeper.

Beside him, Patty snoozed, oblivious to the elemental battle occurring on the Interstate, the strong against the clever, the native against the invader.

The black pickup crept slightly closer to ROSE83's rear bumper as her engine roared. Tim could hear rattles and vibrations from different parts of her through the sound of the engine. He passed the second semi-trailer, one that towed two separate units, almost like a train built for a highway.

---

[10] The lack of a space between rearview and mirror is not a typo, but reflects the wishes of the author, who specified that in the original manuscript. He may be making a reference to the Pearl Jam song on their 1993 album, *Vs.*, whose subject is escape from an intolerable situation.

Something that would only be legal in Nevada, where you only had to make a turn about once every five hundred miles or so.

Tim imagined the black pickup's driver, a tall, powerfully built rancher, looking down at the dented blue car with its effeminate California vanity plate, encased in its UC Santa Zita license plate holder, knowing that the car was from the left coast, a liberal no doubt. He would see the California State Parks bumper sticker that Patty had insisted he put on, though Tim preferred that his car stay unadorned, anonymous, when she traveled to far lands with different customs.

Tim and Patty might run into them later, in a motel parking lot late at night. "Boy," he would say, "why you Californians got to come into our state and get in our way with your slowpoke Jap vee-hickles? That's what you get for not buying American. We don't like your kind round these parts." Followed by a ferocious beat-down, a real country ass-whuppin'. Or maybe his partner, sitting in the passenger seat, might shoot out one of Tim's tires, just for target practice.

They were now almost past the third semi. Tim felt a droplet of sweat trickle down his side, tickling him. They were almost clear, now, there were only four trucks in the convoy. The road was leveling out, too, and for a second Tim saw the speedometer go past eighty.

At the earliest possible moment, Tim's left hand chopped down on the turn signal, and he changed lanes with only the quickest glance to make sure no one was in his blind spot. The black pickup roared past, followed by a retinue of shiny, late-model cars—a metallic blue ovular Taurus sedan, a glistening black Cadillac and some other American-looking cars and SUVs, all seeming to Tim to be emblematic of the places they were going, where people bought only American cars in the colors of red, white and blue and then drove them extremely fast on wide-open highways, unobstructed by speed limits or concerns about the wisdom of consuming fossil fuels.

Tim lifted his foot off the accelerator and let ROSE83 go back to a more comfortable speed. The scary-sounding rattles and vibrations stopped. He patted her on the dashboard. "Sorry, car."

"What," Patty murmured, her eyes still closed.

"I was just talking to ROSE83. I had to drive really fast, to get past these trucks, and I don't think she liked it."

Tim smiled, knowing how kooky this must sound to. Patty opened her eyes for a second, looked at him piercingly, then went back to sleep. Tim looked at the odometer. Ninety miles to Elko. An hour and seventeen minutes to go.

Chapter the Sixth, in which Tim and Patty discuss their Route, and we hear the Story of Melissa

Later that night, after a meal at Denny's and a few pulls on a nickel slot machine in the casino adjoining their hotel, Patty asked, "Where should we go now?" She sat on her motel room bed and leafed through their big Rand McNally road atlas.

"What would you think about going to Boulder, Colorado?" Tim asked in what he hoped was a casual tone.

"That might be cool." Patty traced some highways with her finger, up and to her left. "What about going up to Seattle?"

"Mmm." Tim turned and pondered this. "You want to see Eddie... Patty's in love with Eddie, Patty's in love with Eddie[11]," he chanted.

"Shut up," she said playfully, and threw a pillow at him. "I'm allowed to have a crush."

---

[11] This is most likely another Pearl Jam reference, this time to their lead singer, Eddie Vedder, who was noted for refusing to move to Los Angeles like so many other rock stars, and continuing to live in Seattle.

"Seriously," Tim said, and pondered. "You know, I'm not sure why, but I'm not quite ready to go up to the Pacific Northwest yet. I sort of want to stay in the sun for a while. Anyway, Boulder's supposed to be really cool."

"Okay. I mean, I don't really care. And it would be awesome to be in the mountains."

Now that it was settled, Tim turned away from Patty, glad that she had agreed to go to Boulder first. For Tim had a secret purpose in going there that he hadn't told Patty about yet. It wasn't just that it was a cool college town, though it is. It was that, according to the last he had heard, Melissa lived there.

And who is Melissa? the reader asks. Who is this new character, unrelated to everything that has transpired so far, and why is she important? Why does she keep surfacing in Tim's mind, but not explained? Is she a friend, a past girlfriend? Why does Tim even now make obeisance to her memory and invoke her name like a talisman?

To answer that, we must go back, dear reader, to a strange and different time, the early 80s. 1981, to be precise. A far different world than the one we live in. There are no Macs or Windows PCs, no Nintendo or Sega Genesis. Nor are there cellular phones, fax machines, personal digital assistants, no Internet or World-Wide Web; all of the accoutrements that we now take for granted as the necessities of civilized living. Oh my, no! Instead, here is a world where everything seemed to be either light brown, matte black, or yellow-orange, leftover colors from the 70s mixed with what a few designers at the Sharper Image thought was going to be cool in the coming decade.

However, in the suburban enclave of Palo Alto, CA, it is a good time to be alive, and a very good time to be a kid, provided your parents are professors at Stanford University or work at one of the recession-proof high-tech companies in the area like Xerox, IBM or Hewlett-Packard. In this time, Palo Alto seems a safe, permanently sunny kind of place, wealthy enough to be clean and comfortable, but not so rich that it is antiseptic (the way it is seems to be now, if you have been there recently, it is very sad, to see how it has changed!) or its wealth warped the lives of citizens.

A world of Eichler homes built by the thousands for GIs starting families, and then the houses built in the late sixties and early seventies, full of triangular pieces of glass, sheer wood faces, tile floors and sliding glass doors. Tim's family had moved into one of these kinds of houses in 1977, once his father got tenure at the business school. And, of course, the swimming pool, the amenity that made it a true childhood paradise–sparkling, uncovered, heated to a comfortable temperature by roof-top solar panels.

The Atari 2400 was perhaps the most high-tech device anyone owned, except for those families lucky or far-signed enough to have purchased an Apple II, like Tim's, the device perhaps most responsible for the world we know today.

Parents were tolerant and undemanding, full of the wisdom of Dr. Spock and letting their offspring find their own way, days filled with endless sunlight, video games cost only a quarter, the police were lenient–in short, it was a good time and place to be a kid. Technology was advanced enough to be amusing but not so much that there weren't still many good reasons to go outside. Freedom reigned supreme. Pot was cheap and easily available, sometimes just by swiping a little bit from your parents' stash.

It was in this world that Timothy Page grew up, the quixotic son of a Stanford business school professor and aspiring management consult (no fool, he saw what the future was) and a music teacher who enjoyed fooling around the Apple II that her husband had ostensibly bought for Tim.

Tim, thin with huge oversized brown-rimmed glasses, was perhaps slightly too smart and not quite athletic enough to take full advantage of the circumstances that he had been born into, but he was well served by his quick wits and willingness to be loyal to those he considered worthy. Also, he possessed several key assets for making friends–the above-mentioned Apple II, a house with swimming pool (and diving board!) and a hot tub. Also, he was the undisputed all-time world champion LEGO builder, possessed of a collection that had on many occasions stunned into silence even the most jaded of Palo Alto youth.

Tim belonged to a fairly large loose conglomeration of kids, many of them faculty brats who lived in the Stanford academic, who all played on the same AYSO soccer teams in the fall, caught lizards in the summer, built cities out of LEGO, acted out key scenes from Star Wars, which played the same role to them as the Iliad and Odyssey did to the Athenians and Spartans, in that it was both the ultimate meta-narrative as well as a totalizing belief system, in that there was no philosophical idea or belief that could not be illustrated with events from either *Star Wars* or *The Empire By Strikes Back*.

They all attended Nixon Elementary (named after a beloved local librarian, not the disgraced president, in case you're wondering) a fantastically strange school built by a school system who had perhaps been a little bit too inspired by early-70s Utopian science-fiction movies. The school consisted of four hexagonal "learning pods" connected by corridors to the library, the design and decor an unholy combination of space station and circa 1976 rumpus room, all clad in the ubiquitous chestnut brown, ochre yellow and olive green of the time. If you don't believe me, the school really exists and despite being repainted, retains its original design.

But I digress. Please be forgiving, dear reader. It's all part of the fabric I'm weaving, the edifice I'm constructing, the illusion I'm casting, or whatever.

Anyway, in the summer between fifth and sixth grade, Tim noticed something strange happening to some of the boys in their group. Instead of spending all their time scampering around, building with LEGO and playing pool games, some of them were actually becoming friends with girls–but in a different way than was customary until that time.

Up until that time, girls who liked to play boy games were accepted into the group as honorary boys. Girls who preferred to do girl-type stuff–and there a few, even in liberal, educated Alta Lara–were ignored, or teased mercilessly. Now, though, some of the boys were going off with the girls and being friendly to them, solicitous of them, sometimes even calling them their girlfriends. Had their been a primatologist present, she would have noted that pair bonding had begun to occur.

Tim considered these boys traitors, and swore he would never be interested in girls that way; although curiously, he was quite friendly to the girls who wanted to play his types of games. But it was unthinkable to him that he would someday be one of those boys who had a girlfriend, or kissed a girl. He promised himself that he would never betray himself.

And Tim kept this promise to himself–that is, until he met Melissa.

Melissa Peter: the girl with sun-browned legs who danced on the edge of Tim's dreams. A tough Palo Alto child seemingly born in denim cutoffs and a torn, faded tie-dyed Greenpeace t-shirt handed down from her hippie mother. She was definitely one of the girls who had decided to play boy games when she was a child. Bushy, overgrown brown hair and a bit taller than Tim, since her pubescent growth spurt had already begun, and Tim's, alas, was still some ways away, especially since his mind had begun to change, and it is a hard thing, reader, when such things happen out of step!

She was the daughter of Tim's parents' friends. Her father was a business school professor along with Tim's father. Early in the summer of 1981, Tim's parents decided to hold a beginning of summer pool party. Since they knew Daniel Peter and his wife had kids around Tim and his sister Heather's age, they invited them.

That fateful day, Melissa wore a green and yellow swimsuit, which she had started to out grow, so she wore a pair of torn denim cutoffs over it. While the parents sat on the patio, drinking Henry Weinhard's Private Reserve[12] and exchanging academic gossip, all of the kids gathered in the pool, noisily splashing, jumping and running around, leaving trails of water on the rough pebble patio.

At one point in these games, Tim accidentally kicked Melissa underwater, not very hard, but hard enough in a sensitive area. A few minutes later, while Tim sat on the steps in the shallow end, catching his breath, Melissa came up to him and said, not in an angry way but just with an air of complete and utterly undeniable finality, that if he did that again she would punch him in the mouth. Tim meekly nodded and instantly swam off. From that moment, Tim was utterly and completely captivated by Melissa–but he never admitted it.

The parents, clueless as parents usually and fortunately are about their children, decided that their offspring got along so well that they arranged many other joint family activities in the next few years–baseball games, swim parties, hikes, faculty picnics, and so on. The prospect that Melissa might be present at one of these functions filled Tim with feverish anticipation,

---

[12] A premium brand of domestic lager, popular during the 1980s in the United States.

while at the same time he seemed incapable of admitting that anything was different. His parents watched him bounce around the house on a day when the Peters were coming over, and they wondered why he was even more hyper than usual. His mother asked him what was going on and he responded "nothing" yet inside his mind was racing with images, fantasies, visions of he and Melissa achieving some kind of inchoate union, of him doing things that would inspire her. At first they were just inchoate images of them together, but as he got older they became more specifically sexual.

Ah, who has not felt the first stirrings of young love? The first glance, the first sensation of looking at someone and wanting them? The door opening in your heart and for the first time you realize you would cross half the earth just to spend a moment with the object of your affection. Before Melissa, Tim had never been conscious of needing other people. He didn't mind having friends, but at the same time he was just as happy spending hours by himself creating cities, castles and space stations out of LEGO, vast pixelated primary-colored paradises, with houses, railroads, mountains, fortresses, rocket launch pads, and alien moonscapes. He didn't seek others out, but let them come to him.

But once Tim fell in love with Melissa, all of this wasn't quite enough. He began to wonder what she liked, what excited her; and he was surprised to find that what she liked, started to seem like something he should, too. Melissa had many friends, and some of them were mature for the eighth grade, already drinking beer and smoking pot. Tim, who until this point had probably not imagined that he would drink a beer before he turned thirty, if ever, suddenly found himself intrigued and wanting to do it, too.

Melissa told him many outrageous stories, too, and lest this narratorial aside concentrate too much on Tim's view of Melissa and not enough on her as an actual person, or as actual as a fictional character can be, she derived quite a bit of satisfaction detailing her exploits. In fact, she sort of liked Tim's response, it made her feel like she was quite a bit older than she was. She told him stories of stealing beer from her parents' friends, trying pot with nine-graders when her parents let her go to the Journey concert unescorted. She swore all the time, and the first time Tim ever used the word "fuck" was in her presence, to impress her. For a boy like Tim this was all tremendously exciting. Never was the adage that opposites attract more proved–remember that the next time you scoff at a cliché.

To Melissa, of course, (let's not forget her point of view and let the object be a subject for a while) it was completely obvious that Tim had a severe case of puppy love, but that couldn't be helped. She accepted it as the natural course of events, and was actually surprisingly kind to him considering. Some girls would have either been outrageously cruel to him, or used him, but she did neither. When he was around she was mostly nice, and if he ever started bugging her she just ignored him. When he wasn't, she didn't give him a second, or even a first, thought.

Now, you're saying, this is just an entirely typical case of first love, and so what? The problem was, instead of Tim's first crush lasting a few months, fading, then being replaced with other, more plausible crushes that in fits and starts would eventually become real relationships, something in Tim's mind went awry. Tim's love for Melissa remained in his mind and increased with the passing months (and years) instead of lessening. It was a wound that refused to heal, a hole that couldn't be filled. It was as if Tim's mind has gotten itself into an endless loop and could never get out of it.

Throughout high school, no other girls interested him the way Melissa did. It wasn't until he reached UC Santa Zita that he met a girl who made him temporarily forget Melissa, but he realized later that she was just a temporary substitute, a reflection, and that his love for Melissa remained just as strong. In the deepest part of his mind, he was sure that some day he would blossom, shed the outer skin that he wore and become the kind of guy who could meet Melissa on her own terms. But this prospect always lay far in the future.

Can a story like this have a happy ending? Very rarely. What's a happy ending, anyway? If this novel ended with Tim actually getting Melissa; his foolish, obsessive infatuation rewarded completely at odds with the fundamental nature of male-female relationships, then what good is that?

Tim learned to deal with his love, the way a functioning alcoholic learns to deal with always feeling hung-over when they're not drunk. After he went to college he started to have a real life again—with one exception. He never fell in love with anyone else; or, more accurately, he never let himself fall in love. He did feel some attraction to other girls, and a few girls fell for him in a big way, but nothing ever came of it. Tim remained as virginal as he was on that long ago June day when he had sat with Melissa on the pool steps and she had threatened to punch him in the mouth.

All this being said, the only person Tim had ever told all the truth to was Patty. There was something about their friendship that enabled Tim to say whatever he felt to her; he never thought about it first. But it was a relief for him to talk about it after so many years. When he had finished telling her the story, she simply nodded and said, "Oh, that explains a lot, I guess" and said no more about it.

There it ends, another promising literary work undermined by pointless nostalgia. I don't remember why I stopped writing "Conquistador." The idea of a temp being like a knight errant, roaming the country and righting wrongs, is a semi-decent one and I probably should have focused on that, instead of getting distracted with all of the Tim back-story, which regurgitated material I had already explored in Notes For a Future Novel, *even if in some ways I think the flashback is better executed technically, and more vividly written. Once that happened, I got bore with it.*

I remember reading a writer's response to the question "Where do you get your ideas?" like ideas are some rare and precious thing. His response was that he had ideas all the time, the trick was figuring which ones were worth pursuing. Sometimes you have an initial idea that ends up leading you to another place entirely, like what happened with me and 1989/Celebrated Summer. That's a good thing, and the reason that writing can be a worthwhile activity despite the short hours and pleasant working conditions.

"Conquistador," unfortunately, is an example of getting distracted from a good idea and getting mired in rehashing an old one. Balancing the discipline of sticking with an idea despite it being difficult, against letting that idea evolve into a new and better one, is one of those subtle things you can only learn by long years of experience, and it's one of the reasons I think that writing is such a late-blooming profession.

We now enter a long gap of In Search of Narrative, *with no selections between 1995 and 2000. In the fall of 1995 and early I worked on a project called* Scenes From the J-Church *(If I ever publish a collection of my screenplays, I will include it as part of the bonus materials) which was another attempt to document my life of the time, of living in San Francisco, partying, going to see live music, getting seduced by the tech industry, and watching as my friends became involved in long-term relationships and settle down. As with everything else I wrote post-DSW, it didn't quite sustain my interest. I was still searching for that project, which would be, if not my magnum opus, a work that would take my career to the next level.*

Spring 1996, of course, finally brought a work that became my new primary focus of my creative energy, *1989 A Novel*, later titled Celebrated Summer. *I wrote a tremendous amount of spring 1996 to early fall 1997, probably the most productive period of my life since I had been living in Seattle.*

In fall 1997, though, I stopped working on it. In fact, I decided to stop writing altogether. The reasons for this are complex, though really quite simple. I was feeling frustrated with my life, and I had a great hunger for recognition and achievement. I felt like my writing hadn't really caught on like I would have liked. I was desperate to fall in love and feel the happiness and social stability that my friends seemed to enjoy. While I had dreamed that artistic creation might lead to love, I was up until that point a Master forever in search of his Margarita.

At the same time, the Dotcom boom was accelerating and it seemed like everyone was joining a startup and getting rich. I decided on a new life plan—work for a startup, moonshot IPO, buy my own island, and then spend the rest of my life working on my writing. I also thought professional success might help me with the ladies.

Alas, it didn't turn out that way. And my hiatus only lasted until fall 2000. Even during the heady days of 1999 and 2000, I still found myself daydreaming about 1989. The characters stayed with me, and I knew that I had to revisit that world and find some kind of closure. I wasn't quite ready, though, to dive back into it, so I did work on a few other things, including the next two selections.

First was "Personal Brand", which I first conceived of in October 2000 while attending a wedding of two friends in Sonoma. As you might expect, it was inspired by my experiences in Dotcom (or Dotbong, as my friend and mentor Joe Mahoney called it.) It showed how the language of business and marketing was starting to infect people's lives and how they thought about themselves, a trend which has continued unabated in the decades since. There are elements of the story, of course, which I lifted from the company I worked for, such as the relationship between the EVP of Marketing and the CEO.

Personal Brand

"I'm all about presentation. On a going forward basis, of course."

Hallie turned, surprised, to face the source of this remark. It had sounded like Stacy, one of the web coders, but the statement had been so impersonal and authoritative it couldn't possibly be her. But it was, standing with a cup of coffee in one hand and a book in the other, Stacy's pointed face jutting out at Hallie.

Plain, sharp-faced, and unremarkable, Stacy was one of five html coders employed by DateConnect.com. She reported to Hallie, as did the other four. Stacy was by far the most mediocre of them—not incompetent enough to fire, but one Hallie would never trust with an emergency fix on the live site, especially if it were one for a bug found by DateConnect.com's insomniac CEO, who could always be trusted to always find the most serious bugs at the most inconvenient times.

Hallie had become skilled at dealing with these late-night emergencies—coordinating her html coders and DateConnect's one hapless engineer (all of the others had left the month before when the company had finally canceled its much-delayed IPO) by making calls and prioritizing work on her cell phone while simultaneously holding a beer, smoking a cigarette and straining to hear through the chatter of non-dotcom friends telling her to throw her cell phone in the toilet.

Stacy, though, was never the one she called in those situations. Instead, she got the pointless updates to the marketing pages of the brochure site that Hallie only did to appease the EVP of Marketing and prevent a complete breakdown of relations with her.

"Great," said Hallie. She took a sip of coffee, trying to take her mind off the urge she felt to smoke a cigarette–an urge which had presented itself in her mind the moment she had heard Stacy's strangely altered voice.

"My core brand value is all about getting shit done," Stacy said, with preternatural confidence and a slight emphasis on the next to last word, to let Hallie know that dropping a four-letter word in a casual conversation with her superior was her way of emphasizing just how committed she was to the idea.

"Cool," Hallie said. Her Palm Pilot beeped. Hallie took it out, glanced quickly at the blinking meeting reminder, and caught Stacy staring at it with an almost animal-like hunger. Hallie forced a smile, and quickly put her Palm back in her pocket. She had a meeting with the Executive Vice-President of Marketing, who didn't like to be kept waiting.

"The key takeaway is that it's not consistent with the brand. I'll have to talk to Peter," said the EVP of Marketing, a deceptively good-looking woman of about forty. She and Peter, the CEO, had a strangely tight but conflict-ridden relationship, which reminded Hallie of one of those couples that nobody else liked to be around, because either they were arguing viciously with each other or united in fighting with everybody else. When they disagreed, Hallie had learned to step aside until they hashed it out. This appeared to be one of those times.

Peter was a brilliant, but utterly random, person. When he wanted something done, his habit was to simply go to the nearest person who could execute his request; org chart and reporting relationships be damned. The EVP, on the other hand, was utterly devoted to process and hierarchy. Hallie was sympathetic to the EVP, since much of Hallie's time was spent learning about strategic initiatives from her coders. Considering she was DateConnect's Executive Producer–a grandiose title that sounded great if you thought it meant the same thing it did in Hollywood–it seemed like she should know first. But Hallie had learned not to let things like that bother her too much.

Hallie had forgotten about the conversation with Stacy until this moment. With a sinking sensation, she faced the EVP and forced her face into a noncommittal expression.

"I don't know," Hallie said slowly. "I'll try and find out."

"Do that," the VP said.

"At least she's been getting to work earlier," Jay said. Having the most organization skills in the company, other than Hallie, Jay was now the de facto production manager for the site. DateConnect's web production department occupied a row of cubicles along the western wall of the large open space that formed DateConnect's offices, a typical San Francisco South of Market office space–large, high ceilings, reinforced brick outer walls. DateConnect's CEO was, among other things, a *feng shui* devotee, the result of several years he spent in Hongkong in the 1980s. Thus, the office had been laid out according to strict *feng shui* principals–growing plants but never cut flowers, dog-legged corridors so evil spirits would get lost, and fountains in each of the large spaces four corners. DateConnect had only two proper offices along the northern wall, which were occupied by the CEO, the EVP of Marketing, the EVP of Engineering and the VP of Business Development.

Jay was smart, driven, and Hallie thought, not likely to stick around DateConnect too much longer, unless their fortunes greatly improved. The job market was so competitive that there was no shortage of companies needing project management skills, especially when they belonged to a person who was also skilled at dealing with people. Had Jay not been around, Hallie probably would have fired Stacy, if only because of her tendency to make Hallie want to smoke every time she opened her mouth. Jay, though, seemed to be able to tolerate her odd personality and extract at least a moderate amount of acceptable work.

"The synergies between my brand and DateConnect's tell me we should be doing more." Peter nodded impatiently and poked his finger urgently on the paper in front of him; one of the documents the EVP of Marketing had distributed at the beginning of the meeting.

DateConnect's model was to both provide its own branded dating service, as well as build match-making services for other websites. So, for example, if there was a African-American portal that wanted a dating component, DateConnect could provide that.

Peter's theory was that the higher the number of people who could find each other, the more likely it was you would find that one special someone you were meant for. He called it the "six degrees of separation" rule and would expound on it endlessly–giving it an almost mystical significance.

Based on this strategy, DateConnect had raised 20 million to hire more engineers as well as a five million dollar ad campaign that, as far as Hallie could see, had succeeded mainly in decorating every single bus in San Francisco with DateConnect's red and white logo. That, and printing everything using the color laser printer, at fifty cents a page.

The company's lone remaining engineer sat in the corner, looking so bored that he quite possibly might have been asleep. He wasn't though, as Hallie saw him take out his cell phone and check something. Probably a voicemail from a recruiter, offering a job, Hallie thought bitterly. She had liked the engineers who had already left–they had been a disorganized, unruly bunch, but at least they had been able to get the job done. To lose the last one would be the final sign the dream was over.

They had built two dating areas for other websites so far, but the problem had been actually getting any money for them. Their first they had to do for free, while the second had in theory been for money, but the customer company had run out of funding, and it was unclear whether DateConnect would ever actually collect. They had offered equity instead of cash, Hallie had heard, which would be like strapping the iceberg to the Titanic, the VP of BusDev had told her in a moment of martini-inspired candor. He had resigned the next day.

"It's the data that's important. We need to have a multiplicity of clients. This is a network effects driven space," Peter said, "and we can't have any barriers to adoption–we should support web, analog phone, PDA, wireless–same data, heterogeneous clients. Remember, we call ourselves DateConnect, but we're really DataConnect."

Hallie saw the engineer roll his eyes, but whether it was in response to this umpteenth repetition of one of Peter's favorite sound-bites, or to the fact that they barely had the resources to keep their existing site running, let alone grandiose projects like creating a client for Palm Pilot or integrating with legacy phone systems, she wasn't sure.

As you can see, I never really pursued the original idea for the story, which was Stacy's quest to improve her personal brand. Instead it just became an opportunity to write down some of my memories of what it was like to work for a faltering Internet startup.

The second of my two Dotcom selections is somewhat more substantial, and indeed is the longest of the pieces I have chosen to include in this compilation. I earlier mentioned Helen of Santa Zita, a novella I created in 1994 based on the Helen-centric portions of Notes For a Future Novel.

During fall of 2000, I took advantage of my Dotcom employer's high-speed laser printer to print copies of all my writing up until that time. I read through them, trying to find something to spark my interest. One of the pieces was that 1994 version of HSZ. That novella's theme of estrangement, of Tim and Helen trying to patch their friendship up after a rocky period resonated with me, since I was coming out of a period when I had many important relationships suffer due to my single-minded devotion to Dotcom. I think that explains why I chose it as my first significant post-hiatus project, instead of getting back into 1989 like I should have.

I may someday rewrite and expand Helen of Santa Zita. However, in case I don't, I am including this, reasonably polished version, based on the draft I completed in spring 2001, but with some passages rewritten for clarity. I present this work with two caveats. First, if you haven't read Celebrated Summer and plan to, it should be noted that Helen of Santa Zita was written with the events of that novel in mind, in fact, much of it was about how Tim and Helen's friendship changed as a result of the events of 1989, so there are spoilers.

The other is that Helen of Santa Zita is not necessarily canonical, at least in terms of the Zitaverse. It's a blend of post-1993 writing and material from Notes For a Future Novel (the scenes from Helen's point of view, obviously) that has been transposed to Santa Zita. There may be inconsistencies in the names of streets and minor characters, and their living arrangements. If so, please accept my apologies.

One last thing: I should thank Anne Green Sonstein for her comments on HSZ, which definitely influenced the version I am

including here. And now, the moment you've all been waiting for—
Helen of Santa Zita, the 2001 novella version.

Helen of Santa Zita

One

Everything was fucked and she had nowhere to go. She couldn't drop out of school. She couldn't get back together with Todd. Helen Zachary took a deep breath and ran her tongue around the inside of her mouth, feeling the burn of the aftertaste of cheap Bloody Mary mix. She was so full of anger. Anger at Todd. Anger at the world. Anger at herself. Anger she could taste on her tongue, like she had just thrown up an entire stomach full of Milwaukee's Best.

She hated the whole ordeal of breaking up and it had been going on for far too long. It had been nearly two weeks since her boyfriend Todd had dumped her. Not only did she not have a boyfriend, but she was also flunking a class and running out of money. Helen wanted to run away–she never wanted to hear the name Santa Zita or stay there another minute; she hated it so much and was so tired of classes, her house and everything else.

Another spasm of tears seized her. Through her smeared vision Helen tried to see how Jessica and Roxy were reacting to this. Were they already dialing the men in white coats to come and drag her away? She couldn't see them, though. Just as well. She squeezed her eyes shut, so tight she started to see stars inside her brain. She sniffed and wiped her eyes for the tenth time with the same tissue. She wadded the tissue up and tossed it to her right, where it landed along with the other tissues she had used that night. She rubbed her eyes with the forefingers of her right and left hands. When she opened them, she could see again. Her friends were not looking at her with disgust and gathering up their things, desperate to escape this house of madness. Instead, they were looking at her with smiles–worry in their eyes, but smiling nonetheless.

"God, I feel so lame about this," Helen said to them. Jessica and Roxy were her two best friends in Santa Zita, and the worst part of all of this was the thought of them seeing her in this incapacitated, disintegrated state.

"Don't worry, Helen. We understand," said Jessica.

"Yeah, totally, we do," said Roxy.

Jessica took another tissue out of the box and offered it to Helen. She shook her head no. She felt better now. She could talk and not sound so broken up. She couldn't stand hearing herself sound that way; so grief-stricken and incoherent.

Helen ran her finger under her lower eyelid, feeling the moist, slimy guck that had accumulated there. She took another tissue from the box Jessica was holding and wiped off her fingers. Her eyes burned, her head throbbed, her stomach ached, and her throat had a lump so large she thought it might choke her. Her contact lenses were too old–they felt scratchy resting on her eyeball and needed to be replaced. Basically, her whole body was falling apart.

"I need some water," Helen said.

She rose and walked to her kitchen. She passed the answering machine. Its red light flashed maddeningly, reminding Helen of everything she had stopped dealing with because of the breakup. Everywhere around her were reminders of disintegration. On the coffee table, hidden from Roxy and Jessica's eyes under a Victoria's Secret catalog, was the mid-term she had just gotten back in Latin American Women Writers. She had gotten an incomplete, which was the PC Santa Zita way of saying "F." As in flunked. Failed. And underneath that was an unexpectedly large credit card bill–the result of an ill-advised trip to Alta Lara Shopping Center she had taken with Gretchen on New Year's Eve. Helen had already given up on the notion of paying off the balance; but now she realized she couldn't even afford the interest payments.

♋

Once she had drunk some water, Helen felt better. Her mouth wasn't so dry and her headache lessened. She heard Jessica and Roxy start talking to each other about the internships they were doing that quarter. Jessica was counseling children in Bakersville who had been displaced by the Yaçoan quake the previous October, while Roxy was a teacher's aid at an elementary school.

"It's been six months since the quake," Jessica was saying. "And they're still living in tents."

"That's fucked," Roxy said.

Yes, it was fucked. The whole world was fucked. How had she ended up in this state? That night had started out well enough. Despite her depression, Helen was eager to reconnect with her friends. She had been neglecting them, she knew, and she missed their company, and advice. The excuse for getting together had been to study and then watch *Roseanne* and *Thirtysomething*, but before and after there had been much opportunity for gossip and chit-chat. To Helen's relief, Roxy and Jessica were sensitive enough to not interrogate her about the break-up–Roxy's sole comment had been "you seem to be doing pretty well, all things considered".

It had been wonderful to sit, drink the Bloody Marys Roxy made, and listen to gossip about their friends who lived on the east side of Santa Zita–Tina and Stravinsky not-so-secretly dating, partying with Peter and the two Jakes, Torrance nearly getting busted selling weed at Beachhouse Brewing–but every

CHRIS ERNEST HALL

time Helen relaxed, a voice inside her reminded her of what had happened, that Todd had rejected her and that, superficial circumstances aside, everything was not okay and she was, ultimately, fucked. Drinking more Bloody Marys had seemed to be a good way to quiet that voice, but it hadn't worked. Instead, the voice seemed to be getting louder and more insistent, drowning the voices of her two friends.

Helen had started drinking faster and more frequently, hoping that if she drank enough, she would pass beyond care, but that hadn't happened. She just thought about him more, and it got harder and harder to hold back the raging storm of grief pouring out of the black hole within her–the fear that anything good in her life could be taken away at any time.

As Helen started in on her fourth Bloody Mary, Jessica had decided some music would help cheer her up. She selected the Steely Dan greatest hits tape they had made at the end of the previous summer. Unfortunately, that was the one artist that reminded Helen of both of the serious boyfriends in her life, and consequently the absence of them both and the improbability that she would ever fall in love again, leading to the inescapable conclusion that she was destined to die alone.

Her first serious boyfriend, David Stone, had been a musician, and Steely Dan had been just about his favorite band in the world. Todd was no musician, and in Helen's humble opinion had very questionable tastes in music that tended towards the pretentious, but there was one particular Steely Dan song that was inextricably linked in her mind with their relationship, with the one single moment when their hearts and minds had been in accord, when their commitment to each other had been complete and total. She should have vetoed the selection, but somehow she didn't want to let Jessica and Roxy know how much the music affected her, and that her emotions were not under her control, but subject to the whim of fate.

Relentlessly the tape had marched on as she gulped her Bloody Mary, from "Hey Nineteen to Do It Again," "Peg" and then "Rikki Don't Lose That Number." She should have turned the tape off and put in something else, but she didn't. She just listened to the songs, feeling helpless against the memories that erupted in her brain.

Jessica and Roxy chattered on and on, their conversation about classes, internships and future plans seeming more and more at odds with the way the world truly was, which was a cold unfeeling place where everyone was ultimately alone.

Finally, when that song–*their* song–had come on, the floodgates had opened and all self-control was lost. Helen remembered that feeling of closeness, her victory over masculine reserve and fear of commitment, when they had held each other during the song, stroking each other's hair, and Todd had confessed he loved her and only her, that his life was better with her in it.

On X the guitar solo had seemed to last forever, cycling over and over into itself–the perfect sound for the perfect moment. Tonight, though, the melancholy lyrics had seemed to say more to her than the music. *Your ever-lastin' summer is fadin' fast.*

Before she even knew it, tears were pouring out of her eyes, drenching her cheeks, and her breaths became audibly ragged. Jessica stopped in mid-sentence and Helen had collapsed against her, her chest quaking with sobs. Helen tried to apologize between sobs and cries of anguish, as Jessica and Roxy endlessly repeating words of comfort. It had been quite the scene; just about the biggest spectacle in Santa Zita history; with Helen as the star attraction.

Now that the storm had passed, Helen contemplated what was going to come next. But what was she going to do? What could she do? Anything? Helen felt her eyes sting, as if her eyes were trying to water up again but the tear ducts were too dry to produce anything. She clamped her eyes shut, placed her hands on the side of the sink and inhaled again, trying to fill her lungs without her breath catching in her throat. The glass she was refilling with water overflowed. Helen jammed the tap off. It leaked. No matter how hard she pushed it, a trickle of water seeped out and plopped into the mottled metallic sink. Helen lifted the glass, drank several swallows, and refilled it again. She turned around and went back to the living room.

"The teacher said she would write a recommendation for me," Jessica said to Roxy as Helen re-entered the room. Her two friends looked up at her but said nothing, as if she were so fragile a single unexpected sound might cause her to shatter into a million little pieces. Helen smiled wanly, trying to show them she was stronger than they thought.

Before she sat, Helen gathered the damp, snotty tissues lying on the reddish-pink couch, crumpled them up in a ball and carried them to the bathroom. She dropped the wad of tissue onto the top of the pile of trash in the Zambiggini's grocery bag they used as a garbage can, so it just rested on top. She rinsed off her hands and rejoined Jessica and Roxy. When she sat, Jessica reached over to her and gave her a quick hug.

"Okay," Helen said. "Okay. This is so ridiculous," she said, and shook her head. "You know, I never told you the story of how Todd and I finally broke up."

"We were wondering," Roxy said, "but... well, you know. I thought you'd tell us when you were ready."

"Tell us now," Jessica said gently, but insistently.

"Well," Helen said, and took a deep breath. "We hadn't hung out for several days. I don't know why, I guess I was tired of him, and I had been thinking that we should end it for several weeks. Ever since I got back from San Diego, it hadn't been the same. It hadn't been the same since last December."

Both Jessica and Roxy nodded soberly.

"The last time we had been together," the weekend before, "had been an absolute disaster. We went to a party at his friend Willoughby's house."

"That guy," Roxy said, and rolled her eyes.

"Before we went, I told Todd I would drive so he could drink as much as he wanted. So, we were at the party, and I only drank two beers and he knew it—while he had at least three, and probably four, by the time I told him I wanted to go. He wanted to stay, but I had a headache and there was no one there for me to talk to—just surfers and their slutty girlfriends, who all looked like they were still in high school. And knowing Willoughby, they probably were."

As soon as she said that, though, she wished she hadn't. She had meant merely to underscore to Roxy and Jessica that she knew how lame Todd and his friends were, but in doing so she had inadvertently reminded Jessica of their friend Tim, and the argument they had had when Jessica found out he was dating April, a girl who was still in high school.

"Willoughby," Roxy said, shaking her head. "He's going to end up in jail, one of these days."

"Why are men like that? Jessica asked. "Don't they understand how much damage they cause?"

The wounds between Jessica and Tim over that had only recently healed. Jessica had told Helen that she had talked to Tim when she got back to school in January, and that the matter was resolved, but Helen wasn't so sure it would be that easy. Not that Helen on very good terms with Tim, either. His experience with April seemed to have propelled him into a downward spiral that he couldn't pull out of.

"I know. And so I really wanted to leave. I dragged Todd out of there and when we got to my car, he demanded that I give him my keys. He didn't think I was sober enough to drive! I started screaming at him, telling him he was an asshole, and that I had only drank two beers, and he'd had five, and there was no way he was going to drive my car, no way in hell."

"Good," Roxy said. "That put him in his place."

"Well, except that I ended up letting him. I guess I just couldn't stand fighting about it; I already had the most horrible headache, and I just didn't have enough energy to care. The whole way home, I was wishing we would get stopped by the cops, so he'd get totally busted. We came back here, had really lame sex for a while, during which I fell asleep. When he left in the morning, I pretended to be asleep and he didn't try to wake me. After that episode, I didn't feel like seeing him ever again for the rest of my life. On Monday, he called me and left a message. I was screening my calls and I didn't pick the phone up. I just didn't want to. Instead, I said really mean things to him while he talked to the answering service."

Helen smiled at the memory, and then continued. "I told him he sucked in bed and that he had terrible taste in music. That week, he called me every day and left these silly messages, trying to sound all nice and apologetic. Quite frankly, it turned my stomach. Then, Friday afternoon, I came home from school and found a note on the answering machine from Gretchen, telling me there was a message from Todd on the machine that I should listen to. I was like 'oh, another message from Todd, what a bore' but I pressed the button and listened to it anyway. It said: 'Helen, I've been trying to call you all week. You haven't paid me the common courtesy of returning my calls, so I'm going to tell you what I have to tell you now, because I don't know any other way to communicate with you. I think we should break up. Don't call me, and I won't try to call you. Have a nice life, bye.'"

Jessica looked at Helen sadly for a moment, then her lips cracked and a giggle escaped. She laughed out loud.

"Jessica," Roxy said, but then she started giggling, too.

"I'm sorry, Helen," Jessica said, "that's terrible, but it's also funny. It's really funny, tragically funny."

"I know," Helen said, half-laughing, half-crying. "It is. But I felt so humiliated. I had been planning to call him that evening, too. What was his problem? I went four days without calling him, and for that, he dumped me. And he didn't break up with me because we always fought, or that I wouldn't suck his cock, or that we had completely different values. He broke up with me because I wouldn't return his fucking phone calls. There were so many reasons I could have broken up with him that were more legitimate, more real. I never thought he would be the one to break up with me. I thought I would be the one who would pull the plug."

"I think there was more to it than that, Helen," Roxy said.

Of course there was. Helen knew that they knew the battle of not returning phone calls had merely been an absurd denouement to a long, drawn-out ordeal. But she preferred not to think about those other reasons. "I know, but it's still ridiculous. It just makes me laugh, now. I'm not even that angry anymore."

Helen tried to laugh, because it was funny and she wanted Roxy and Jessica to know that she knew it, but she cut it off halfway through when it seemed likely to just turn into more tears. What came out was a sort of strangled half-cough that made her sound like a tuberculoid heroine-victim in a Dickens novel.

"You should forget about him," Jessica said. "You and Todd had your time together, and now it's over. You have to move on. You have a lot more going on in your life than just him."

"I'm trying," Helen said. "I'm trying," but her voice broke, which made her sound as if the attempt had failed even before it began. "I know I got back together with him once before, but I just can't see that happening this time."

Helen hoped that was true. An hour ago, would she have taken Todd back if he had shown up on her doorstep, because it seemed like the only thing that could have ended her pain. That was one thing Helen admired about Jessica, was how she had dealt with Charles, her first serious boyfriend. She had lost her virginity to him, and then gotten summarily dumped just two weeks later.

Jessica been broken-hearted; devastated, even, but she had never tried to get back together with him. She just cut him out of her life. He had called her a month later. From his recalcitrant tone when he asked Helen if Jessica was there, Helen could tell he was having second thoughts, that he might be willing to give it another try. Jessica wouldn't even come to the phone. Helen admired, but also felt wary of, such strength of spirit.

"I have too many other things to worry about," Helen said. "Like my section."

"How's that going?" Roxy asked.

"Shitty. It's becoming a major thorn in my side."

"I thought you liked being a section leader," Jessica said.

"I think I liked the idea. It's just not turning out anything like I imagined it, and my students annoy me. I mean, most of them are okay but there are several hard-core lit geeks who know more than I do, the lesbians hate me because I'm blonde, and Peak is, well, Peak."

Peak, and all that he entailed, was well known to both Roxy and Jessica, who had been in Spanish class with him, and they both made appropriately sympathetic sounds.

"I have thirty papers to grade that my students are all going to want on Friday and I've run out of things to say. I just can't think of an original comment for each one. And most of them are really boring, I have nothing to say about them, so I make stuff up. Or give everyone a good grade, because it's all bullshit in the end."

"Now you know how our professors feel," Roxy said.

"I feel sorry for them, drowning in a mountain of crap. On top of which, I'm not even getting paid for it."

"I thought your TAship was a paid one," said Roxy.

"No... it's really lame. The funding only came through for half of the TAs. Of course, Gretchen and I are only juniors, so we lost out."

"That's fucked," said Roxy. "That's majorly fucked."

"That's terrible," said Jessica. "Can you complain to someone?"

"No, not really," Helen responded. "Joseph told us at the beginning of the quarter, and asked if we still wanted to do it. I thought I could scrape by without getting a job, but... I need money." Helen paused and straightened the pile of catalogs on the coffee table. "And I haven't even mentioned my Latin American Writers class."

"How's that going?" Jessica asked.

"Terrible. It's too early in the morning and I never go. I never read the books. I failed the first mid-term and if I fail the second, I'm up shit's creek with no paddle. I'll fail the class and my financial aid will be cut off."

"Helen... that's really serious," Jessica said. "Will you be able to stay in school?"

"No. I'll have to drop out and get a job. I might have to move back to Montana."

"What?" Roxy said, aghast. Jessica said nothing, but she looked at Roxy and nodded slightly, as if their worst fears had been confirmed.

"That's terrible," Jessica said. "You can't go back to Montana. Even if you drop out, you can still stay here."

"You can crash here with Tina and I," Roxy said. "We can't lose you, Helen. We need you here."

"I know, but..." Helen let her cheeks fall and looked at Jessica. She smiled and squeezed Helen's hand, while Roxy thin, strong fingers did the same to her shoulder. In spite of herself, Helen found their reactions reassuring–at least someone cared where she ended up.

"You can still pass the class," Roxy said. "There's time."

"I really loved that class when I took it last year," Jessica said. "Maybe we could study together."

"That would be great," Helen said. "I could really use the help."

"How about Saturday night?"

"Okay, cool," Helen said. She was amused at herself–as recently as last fall, she would have regarded studying on a Saturday night as a catastrophic failure of her social life, but now it seemed plausible–possibly even a good idea. It was certainly a relief not to have to come up with a plan, because there really wasn't anything she wanted to do.

Jessica smiled, then yawned quickly and quietly. "You guys, I need to go to bed. What about you, Roxy?"

"Yeah, I need to get home, too, get some shut-eye. Hopefully Jake and Mick won't be making too much noise."

Jessica and Roxy both stood. Helen walked with them to the front door.

"Hey, Helen, you want to meet for coffee on Thursday?" Roxy asked.

"Totally," Helen said. "I'll be at Fremont College between noon and one."

Helen hugged both of them, said good night, and watched as they walked down the staircase to the ground. She looked up and saw the low clouds overhead, their gray rumbled bottoms lit burnt orange by the city lights. There were no stars to look at, so Helen started to shut the door.

Just as it was almost closed, a small beige creature shot in and disappeared into the kitchen. Helen closed the door and sighed. In the kitchen, she heard a sequence of pathetic mews. Her almost full-grown kitten, Bristle, was hungry.

She went in the kitchen, where Bristle was pacing in front of her empty food and water dishes, her tail sticking straight up as she meowed desperately. She had been outside all day.

"Okay, you silly creature. Here's some food. I can't believe how much you eat."

Helen went to the pantry and got out the cat food bag. She poured Bristle's bowl full of the little red-brown stars that smelled like over-ripe cardboard. As soon as she placed it back on the floor, Bristle began purring and ravenously inhaling her food. Helen filled her water bowl with tap water and set it down next to the food. She stroked the cream-colored patch on Bristle's back and felt her lithe body buzzing.

As she returned to the living room, she glanced at the red lights of Gretchen's clock radio in the darkness of her room. She was amazed to see that it was past one in the morning. She needed to sleep. She had to meet with Joseph Harkes at eleven the next morning, and teach section at two. She had promised Joseph that she would have her section's papers to return to them after lecture. That was one of the things she was supposed to get done tonight which had been pre-empted by her emotional collapse. It was going to be very hard to explain that to Joseph, though, without making her seem more vulnerable in his eyes than she really wanted.

Helen went in the living room and sat back on the couch, staring at the front door. Her housemates showed no sign of returning. It was just as well. Even though she felt weird being alone in the house, she didn't really want to see her housemates either. She thought about trying to read, but her eyes felt too worn out and she gave up after several sentences. Now that the tears had dried and stopped lubricating her contact lenses, she could feel them resting uncomfortably on her eyeball. Add that to the list of things she had to deal with–new contacts. While she was at it, she could also add it to the list of things she couldn't possibly afford.

A few minutes later, Bristle joined Helen in the living room. Bristle walked up to her, tensed her haunches like she were going to jump on Helen's lap, but then snapped her head around and began biting her lower back. She did this several times, and then scratched with her hind legs repeatedly.

"Oh, Bristle. You've been outside all day and you're covered with fleas."

Helen got down on her knees and studied Bristle's coat. She saw the tiny blood-sucking creatures, jumping maniacally among her short hairs.

"Poor thing. I'll buy you a flea collar tomorrow, I promise."

Helen got up and went to her bedroom, preparing to sleep alone.

The squeak of the door opening woke Helen. Her roommate Gretchen was home. That quarter Jessica had the single; not that it was doing her much good. She hadn't dated anyone since Ellery the previous summer, and seemed a bit bummed about it.

Helen used to miss having her own room because it made romping with Todd so much more convenient—in her own bed, with at least somewhat clean sheets, instead of at Todd's or some other random location. Helen remembered her first fall quarter in that situation with pleasure. The second hadn't been quite as thrilling—sex with Todd had come to seem more like a chore than a pleasure, but she liked the nights alone with no Todd and no worries about when to go to bed, and whether she would wake Jessica up.

Helen heard the quick, whispered "shit" as Gretchen's foot hit the corner of her bed. Helen rolled over, put her covers over her head. Now she just missed having her privacy. She,

Jessica and Lana had always gone to bed around the same time, or Helen had gone to bed before either of them, so it hadn't been so bad. Gretchen, though, was prone to late nights at the Cyclops Eye and other dive bars, drinking with her weasel-faced and snake-hearted boyfriend, Bill. Helen lived in dread of his visits, of having to hear his snide, derisive tone directed at their house, UC Santa Zita, and especially Gretchen. Worse, Bill's friend Frank frequently tagged along–a brutish oaf who had conceived an infatuation with Helen that would have been amusingly ludicrous if he wasn't so terrifyingly large and lacking in self-control.

Helen tried to put something else in her mind other than Frank's huge, round face leering down at her, but all she could see was the pile of mail on the coffee table, and the unopened bill on the bottom of it. Maybe she should call her mother and ask for help. No, shine. She hadn't spoken to her mother since right after the quarter started. Her mother had troubles of her own, like an alcoholic ex-boyfriend whom she had been trying to get the local police to enforce a restraining order against him–difficult since the ex-boyfriend and the sheriff were drinking buddies. There was also lingering resentment over Helen's having spent Christmas with her father. Her mom had been pissy about that, which always drove Helen crazy. One Christmas with her father; the first one with him since she had been a small girl. Helen knew that her father was making an effort; and a free trip to San Diego was a free trip to San Diego. The weather there sure beat Hamilton, Montana. The bitterness that remained between her parents amazed Helen, and she hoped she never saw anything like it in her or any of her friends.

A soft wheezing from the direction of Gretchen's bed told Helen she was already asleep. Even when she was drunk, Gretchen didn't snore–thank goodness for small favors. Jealous that Gretchen had already reached the oblivion she was desperate for, Helen searched her mind for something pleasant to think about it, something to look forward to.

Drawing a blank, Helen turned over again and tried to think of nothing at all. Nothing at all. Just like the characters in that vapid novel by Brad Eastman Aaronson, surrounded by sports cars, coke, and too much money. Santa Zita was like the LA in *Nothing At All*, only with redwoods and bong hits instead of palm trees and cocaine–and too little dough instead of too much. Helen felt herself smile. That was such a Tim idea. She missed him. They needed to hang out. She was going to have to make the first move with him. She had been pissed at him for not calling her back when she called him the day after Todd dumped her. Maybe she should apologize to him, though he didn't really deserve it. She had to do something.

Two

As Helen walked down the Humphrey College colonnade, she saw a flyer with several red hearts advertising a dance at Redwood College. Seeing the flyer reminded her that Valentine's Day was only a week away. How fucking typical that she had broken up with Todd right before that oh-so-wonderful day. To Helen, Valentine's Day was cursed–she had never really had a good one.

Her freshman year she had expected to get something from David (a card, flowers, a phone call–she wasn't sure what, but *something*), and got... nothing. After some tears in Roxy's room, her friend went and "borrowed" a bottle of Jack Daniels from Davey and Pete, inspired by some man troubles of her own. That night had ended with her in the moat, yakking her brains out–Jake on one side of her and Mick on the other, holding her up so she wouldn't pass out in a puddle of her own vomit. Thank God Jake had been there–she wasn't sure she would have trusted Mick alone in that situation. Not that she actually remembered any of this, of course. It had been retold (and recreated) enough times in the next two years that Helen knew she would never be allowed to forget it.

A year ago she had boycotted Valentine's Day, since she was still officially broken up with Todd (if not unofficially sleeping with him, and even more unofficially wishing they were back together.) Tim had made her dinner at his place in the Kane-King Apartments (chicken stir-fry, rice, and some surprisingly classy white wine he had inexplicably acquired). Here it was a year later, and she was broken up with Todd again, this time without the comforting thought that if she had really wanted to, she could have him back,

Helen wondered if she should call Tim and ask him to do something that night. Would it be too obvious if she called him and suggested doing something on Wednesday? During the past year, Tim had become sensitive about serving as a substitute boyfriend. Helen didn't have much patience with Tim on that point. Sure, he would probably rather be with the love of his life–wouldn't they all? But if you weren't, shouldn't you do something fun, instead of sitting around brooding, which seemed to be Tim's preferred way of dealing. Life was short, wasn't it? Why not make the most of it?

There was also the possibility of doing something with Gretchen. Her housemate, though, was utterly unreliable in these matters; prone to agreeing to do something and then flaking at the last minute at the Bill's behest. Jessica and Roxy were more reliable, but they were sufficiently PC and, Helen sighed to herself, empowered, that they probably would have considered actually doing something special on Valentine's Day an embarrassing sign of weakness. She could imagine asking them about it, hearing them sniff and say they were going to study together and "oh is it Valentine's Day that night? I had no idea." Tim seemed like her best bet. The only question was how to broach the subject. She had better just hang out with him first, and bring it up at the right moment–it wouldn't work if she just called him out of the blue and proposed it.

As Helen passed Natural Sciences, a huge yawn split her face and nearly made her collide with a pack of giggling fresh-people. She had not gotten nearly enough sleep the night before. This walk, which she had done a thousand times before, was just not stimulating enough to keep her awake.

When Helen had first come to UCSZ, she had loved the long paths through the woods, meandering through the towering redwoods and crossing each other at random, making it seem more like a nature park or summer camp than a university campus. Sometimes it had been more fun to walk to the other colleges, drunk and stoned, searching for mythical three-keg ragers–passing through the mists, hearing the endless drip drip drip of condensation from the hanging mosses, breathing in the smell of moist growing, and catching brief glimpses of dark yellow from a banana slug–than actually going to the parties themselves.

Now, though, the winding path just seemed tiresome, like someone had intentionally inflicted it on her just to waste her time, to make even the simple act of getting from one obligation to another a massive chore. Someone had told her the government had designed UC Santa Zita this way, to make it hard for students to gather in one place and protest. She believed it.

The path finished its meandering and Helen stepped onto the second bridge of her journey. Something caught her eye, and for a moment she thought she saw Todd. It wasn't him, though, just another six-foot guy with short black hair. This one wasn't as good-looking as Todd, though.

Helen dreaded the possibility of running into Todd, either on campus or worse, at some party. They still had enough mutual friends that it was likely she would see him at some point. Their groups were pretty separate, but there were connections. Torrance, for one.

She had no idea what it would be like when they did. It was going to happen, she knew. UC Santa Zita was sufficiently spread out that, unless it was freshmen year and you were all living in one dorm, you weren't going to see people every day, but you would run into them eventually. She hoped, no, she resolved, that it would be adult encounter, that they would both be mature, civil, but not friendly.

The prospect of running into him randomly, though, was sufficiently stressful that Helen wondered if she should preemptively hang out with him, just to get it out of the way. Maybe they could go get coffee at Cafe Nightingale. That might be okay. They could just talk and clear the air. Helen saw them in her mind, at a table in one of the back rooms, where no one was likely to see them. He was telling her that he was wrong to make her go through what she did alone. He should have gone with her, he wished with all his heart he had. He just hadn't been ready to deal with the reality of the situation. But he knew there could be no forgiveness for what he had done. He told her what she wanted to hear, and she felt herself forgiving him. They walked out of Cafe Nightingale and he offered to walk her home. When they got there, both Gretchen and Jessica were gone.

Realizing that her thoughts of Todd were starting to turn into a fantasy of them getting back together was almost enough to make Helen hurl herself off the bridge. Todd was like some awful venereal disease, which you could treat but never actually cure, like herpes. She could cover him up in her brain, but he was always there lurking under the surface.

Maybe she should just kill him. That might be better. There was a finality about it that pleased Helen. When you got right down to it, Todd just didn't deserve to live. If they listened to her story, no court could possibly convict her. Helen smiled to herself. The only question was how, and when. She stared down through a hole in the bridge's wooden slats; a brief reminder that she was not on safe pavement, but actually a hundred feet in the air. She heard the chatter of some students on bikes below, debating whether they should continue up the ravine, or up the hillside.

♋

Stepping onto the third bridge forced Helen to think about her meeting with Joseph. She was not looking forward to it. Partly because she hadn't finished evaluating her sections' papers yet, something she had promised would be done the last time they had met. But also because her meetings with Joseph exhausted her, as she tried to follow his interminable monologues and obsessed over every single word and gesture he made.

Helen was always on her guard with Joseph. He had a reputation around campus as a womanizer who wasn't averse to fooling around with his graduate students and teaching assistants. Helen might have been able to dismiss them as just gossip if she hadn't actually seen Joseph and Theresa scamming in a restaurant in Alta Lara.

Before she left for Spain, Jessica had told Helen she shouldn't even consider working for a professor capable of such monstrous errors in judgment. Helen agreed with Jessica that Joseph's conduct was inappropriate. It wasn't just that he was older than them. Professors were part of a different world—they were teachers, and should be role models as well. Joseph had crossed a line he shouldn't have crossed, just like Tim had crossed a line he shouldn't have crossed when he went after April, that high school girl he had worked with at the movie theater, while he had been cashier and assistant manager. It had been the summer of authority figures abusing their power. So what else was new? The world was a fucked up place. But she had never thought of Tim as someone who was going to add to that—it wasn't like him, and it made her sad to think that he had betrayed what he stood for.

During fall quarter she had seriously considered telling Joseph she didn't want to be his TA after all, but she hadn't. She was just too reluctant to let a plum like that fall through her hand. She still had hopes (growing fainter by the day, of course) of attending graduate school, and teaching a section in an upper-division class; usually the job of graduate students, would be invaluable experience to have when applying.

She had other reasons as well. She had been eager to teach the section, to prove her intelligence matched her physical beauty. She had started to wonder if her life was becoming too much about her looks. But now that she was a month into it, she wondered if she had gotten in over her head. It had seemed easy to think of things to say when she was just one of thirty voices, and it didn't really matter if she spoke up or not. She had done well in Contemporary American Fiction, but she was forced to admit that a lot of it was due to Tim and Jessica. They had studied together, written papers together, filled each other in on what they hadn't read. Jessica let Helen read her notes, and Tim had offered his as well, but they were written in an indecipherable scrawl that he cheerfully admitted not even he could read. The three of them had gotten in the habit of pulling outrageous all-nighters, fueled by beer, coffee, and herbal tea.

Tim seemed to delight in waiting until the last possible moment, then writing his entire paper in one burst on Helen's typewriter, even though he had a perfectly good computer and printer in his room at the Kane-King apartments. Then he would get excellents on them, which irritated Helen to no end. Nobody who wrote a paper in a single eruption of bullshit should be allowed to do so well on it. Once he finished his, he would type or retype hers, often rewriting it in the process. Her best paper had been based on an idea he had randomly tossed out at Claimstake when they had gone there to study. His idea was about California and what it represented in *China Men, Nothing At All,* and *Crazy For Love,* three novels that superficially had nothing to do with each other. Tim said California represented the end of dreams–the place where people had to confront themselves and who they really were. He had already decided what he was going to write on, so when Helen asked if she could steal his idea, he shrugged and said yes. It had ended up being the best paper she had written at UCSZ.

Although Tim procrastinated (rhymes with masturbated, Helen thought to herself with a smile) on his papers, he always did the reading. Helen sometimes wondered why Theresa hadn't recommended Tim to be a section leader. She thought maybe it was because Tim, though he always had something interesting to say, could be obnoxious and intolerant of ideas that he disagreed with. Most of the time he restrained himself, but every so often he would lose it and crush someone else's idea with a sarcastic remark. Theresa liked Tim, but she also had to reign him in every so often, remind him that he was just one student of thirty, not the second coming of Joseph Harkes. Tim seemed amenable to that–he was always responsive to female authority, and seemed to want and expect to be put in his place every so often.

Helen had to admit that despite her trepidation and paranoia, Joseph had behaved himself so far. In deed, at least, if not in thought. There was a gleam of hunger in his eyes that she thought she recognized. He was quite subtle about it, as he would have to be in a place where the wrong word at the wrong time could bring an outcry of sexual harassment and the end of his career, at least at UC Santa Zita. In fact, he was so subtle that even for someone with radar as finely tuned as Helen's, it might have just been her paranoia-fueled imagination.

Helen placed her foot on the first step of the staircase that led up from the bridge into Krupke College. As she passed the Krupke Town Hall, where had she had seen Taj Mahal freshman year and she, Jessica and Tim had taken Philosophy 101 the year before, she checked her watch. She was late; but acceptably so.

"It has been suggested," Joseph was saying, "that the male figures in *China Men* are feminist straw men, meant to primarily represent the false authority of patriarchy, against which Kingston contrasts the genuine thread of discourse and connection that the women create, and in that way maintain, strengthen and affirm the continuity of their culture."

Helen stared at the empty page of her notebook as she struggled to keep listening. Depressed by the straight blue lines with only white emptiness between them, she looked in Joseph's direction. His face was tilted upwards, towards the window, talking to the air in classic academic fashion, as if what was being said were so profound it was more for the benefit of the entire universe than any one particular person.

Joseph had a habit of using expressions like "one might say", "it has been suggested", "some authorities assert", "implicit in the text" or "another way of looking at that is" that made it hard to figure out what he actually thought about anything. Half the time, the hypothetical statements were spoken with an ironic tone that meant, Helen was sure, that anyone who actually thought that was the biggest idiot in the world, if only you were allowed to say such things at UC Santa Zita. Listening to Joseph, Helen sometimes found herself lost in a maze of hypothetical speakers, feeling as if he expected her to sift through all of his various personas and carefully crafted ironies in order to divine what he really wanted her to know. Which, quite frankly, she just didn't have time for.

Some of his irony was accompanied by a thin smile so bitter it seemed self-hating. Joseph didn't feel like the happiest person to Helen. Did he miss Theresa? Wish he were still married? Feel guilty over not having been part of his daughter's life? Helen hoped it was the last. She tried to connect the middle-aged intellectual in front of her with her beer-hazed memories of April from that epic party the previous summer, but failed. Then again, Helen's father, who was compulsively neat and organized, punctual to the second and liked everything run with military efficiency, wasn't much like her. Just another one of God's sick jokes.

Helen frequently found it hard to concentrate in meetings with Joseph, having learned so much about his life that he wasn't aware she knew. His child, the fruit of his loins, had engaged in carnal relations with one of her best friends. It was just all too weird. Such a complicated web of circumstance might be amusing on a yuppie soap opera like *Thirtysomething*, but it was creepy in real life. Couldn't things just be what they were supposed to be? Why did everything in life always have get so tangled up?

"But what they may be ignoring," Joseph continued, "is the sense in which the novel's theme is not the explicit exegesis of those dualities, but rather our need to assemble these dualities in our own act of reading–and interpretation."

With no warning, Joseph turned and looked straight at her. Their eyes locked for a moment, and his gaze was as piercing and direct as his words were subtle and roundabout.

His green eyes regarded her with skepticism, a ghost of a smile on his lips, as if inviting her to share in a private joke. His thought flashed in his mind, as clear as if he had said them out loud: "Although I enjoy forcing you to listen to me pontificate, what would be even better is if you allowed me to fuck your brains out."

After a second of eye contact, Helen turned her eyes towards the window, hoping to see blue. No such luck as grey-white fog still covered the campus. It was going to be one of those days, when the fog never lifts, or finally starts lifting in the late afternoon, just in time for the sun to go down. Helen heard Joseph clear his throat, a short, sharp grunt.

"But that is neither here nor there," he said. "In the academic life, unfortunately, we can not only concern ourselves with ideas. There is also, it has to be said, a regrettable amount of the quotidian as well. For me, but also for you."

Helen nodded, realizing where this was going. She realized how nervous she was about it, that she was perspiring and her lower back ached.

"You said you thought you would be able to return your students' most recent round of papers to them tomorrow?"

"Well," Helen said, "I really wanted to be able to."

Joseph gravely nodded, but said nothing. Helen swallowed, and the excuses she had fabricated earlier vanished from her mind. Her mouth dry, she swallowed several times more, and her heart pounded.

"It's just that the past week has been really busy. Some unexpected stuff came up, and... you know," Helen said, mortified to hear herself making such a pathetic excuse. She might as well tell Joseph the dog ate her homework. She found herself smiling at Joseph–lips parted flirtatiously. He smiled back, an upwards twitching of the corners of his mouth.

"Timely return of the papers is important, Helen. But I know you have many other duties in your life to attend to."

The slight emphasis Joseph put on the word "duties" made Helen think of sex for some reason, as if he were aware and sympathetic that the reason she hadn't finished evaluating the papers was her grueling schedule of frequent and varied copulation. Helen couldn't figure out if it was her derangement or his that made her read so much into his words.

"There is another set of papers due... tomorrow?" Joseph asked. Helen nodded. "Indeed," Joseph said. "Indeed."

Their eyes met again, and Helen, unable to think of anything else to do, smiled at him. He smiled beneficently back.

"Well, I had better get back to my own version of the quotidian. See you at two o'clock."

Irritation filled her at all this absurd subtext. Helen stood and slung her backpack around her left shoulder. She muttered a quick "bye" and hurried out of the office. Every time she thought she couldn't sink any lower, she did. She felt unclean, as if she and Joseph had just been intimate. As Helen passed by the ground-floor apartments she kept her head down, as if she were afraid she might be recognized, even though she didn't know anyone who lived at Krupke College.

Three

Helen tossed her book aside on the couch, folded her arms, and yelled "Fuck!... this!" at the ceiling. She had just made her one hundred and seventy-ninth attempt to get past the first page of *Las Mujeres de las Nubes*, and failed. The novel was written in language so flowery, and elliptical that it might as well have been in the original Spanish for all the sense Helen could make out of it.

She wished she were PMSing so she could blame that for her irritation, instead of her life, but her period was still at least a week away, and she was forced instead to contemplate lack of Todd, her ineptitude as section leader and imminent academic meltdown as the source of her grouchiness. Not having Todd in her life irritated her. Being sad because of it made her even more annoyed.

Helen knew that she would never get through the book left to her own devices. Like working out, some things had to be done with another person or it would never happen. Only the threat of losing face could compel her to continue on. She remembered Tim, and her plan for Valentine's Day. To set the stage for that, maybe they could go study at Claimstake. They had done that many times the year before. Time to kill two birds with one stone.

She needed to give him a chance to show he was over what she had said to him at Peter's birthday party. It was the first Friday night of the quarter, at Jake and Peter's apartment in Dead Oak. Tim had showed up, and everyone had been really psyched since he had been so MIA the previous quarter, and had even shined the epic end of the 80s New Year's Eve party at Sarah Wolfe's house in Alta Lara. Despite the fact that he had showed up the party, though, he had seemed moody and out of sorts, angry with everyone and everything.

Helen had gotten more and more irked at him as the party progressed, since everyone was being so nice to him, aware that he'd just had his heart broken, and he seemed only able to be grumpy and irritable in return. She just wanted him to get over it, so they could hang out and he could listen to her problems, instead of caring only about his.

In general, the whole night had irritated her—it wasn't just Tim, but also Jake, Peter and Perse tweaking on speed, watching George being nice to Sophie when Todd Forrest was around, and mean to her when he wasn't, Jamie clinging to Peter like a blood-sucking parasite, and avoiding Sarah Wolfe because she wanted to find out what was going on with Todd Fox, and Helen just didn't want to talk about *that*. Bad vibes all around, and Tim had been the one unlucky enough to push her over the edge.

When it happened, Helen had been drinking beers with he and Jake out on the deck. Tim had, in his best Morrissey-esque moping voice, proclaimed that love was for everyone except him. Jake has asked why he was bumming, and Tim had, instead of saying anything, just looked darkly out into the parking lot as if whatever he was going through was so intense that no words could communicate it. This was more manufactured melodrama than even Helen could stand. "Oh, it's just too many Kane College cardiac injuries," she had blurted out.

She had intended it to be teasing; sharp enough to snap him out of his self-absorption, yet still funny, but it had come out too loud, too cutting–the cruel strike of a harpy's claw. Plus she had said it right in the middle of a pause in the music booming from inside the apartment, so everyone on the deck heard it. Tim had flinched, like he had just been kicked in the stomach, but then he just fixed her with an icy, defiant stare. They didn't say anything more to each other, and Tim left soon after.

Jessica, who had been on the deck with Lana and Roxy at the time, had accused her of being mean in the car ride home. Helen knew it was true, but she didn't like hearing it. And why was Jessica, of all people, defending him? After the way Tim had treated her over the whole April thing, he had no right to have Jessica on his side. She still wasn't sure how Tim and Jessica had reconciled so quickly. Jessica had merely said they had talked, but had been strangely reticent in offering any details. It seemed too easy, and the fact that Jessica didn't seem to want to talk about it only increased her suspicions, like she and Tim had made a secret pact.

So maybe their estrangement was partly her fault. Didn't her breakup with Todd take priority over their stupid tiff? Didn't he understand how hard it was for her? She needed support and all he could do was be pissy. Helen started to get so irritated by Tim that she almost abandoned her plan, but she pushed those thoughts aside. She just had to do it. She had to take the first step.

Helen reached for the phone, trying not to think about all the other people she owed phone calls to. She realized that Tim's number had slipped from her memory. She remembered the first three numbers, but the rest were vague in her mind. She thought there was a seven in there, maybe a two. She had to look at the tattered phone list taped to the wall above the milk crate where the put the beige Princess phone (the same one that she and her mom had used back in Montana, then in Alta Lara) and Gretchen's answering machine.

After two rings, Helen was amazed to hear the phone actually being picked up by a human being.

"Uh, hello?"

"Hey, Tim," Helen said. "What's shakin'?"

"Oh, well..." and Tim paused, as if Helen's question were not merely a routine pleasantry, but demanded serious consideration. "Not much, I guess," he finally said.

Helen gritted her teeth and reminded herself that even at the best of times, Tim had never been one much for telephone conversation. "Do you want to come over and study?" she asked.

"Um... sure," he said.

Helen waited, but Tim said no more. The unnatural pause continued for several seconds before Helen realized she was going to have to take responsibility for arranging the logistics.

"Okay, well, just come on down. In your car," she added, in case that detail escaped Tim's attention.

"Right," Tim said. "I'll be down soon."

Helen hung up the phone and took a deep breath. Any doubts she'd had about the evening ahead had not been allayed by their conversation. She glanced back at the phone list. She had blacked out Todd's number with an indelible marker, but the numbers could still be seen, ghost-like. She thought about tearing up the phone list and just making a new one, but it seemed like too much work. Instead, she rose and went back to the kitchen, wondering if there was anything that she could scrape together to make a filling meal with.

While Helen waited for Tim to arrive, she sat at her kitchen table and idly leafed through the latest Victoria's Secret catalog. They were now getting five copies a month—two to Helen, one to Helen's old housemate Lana and two to mysterious people who had lived in the house previously. She thought about how silly most of the models looked, clad only in garters and low-cut translucent bras, but also wearing black horn-rim glasses and tying their hair primly back, as if they were lawyers and doctors who dressed up as high-priced call girls in their spare time.

In an attempt to get in a positive frame of mind, Helen made herself recall the good times with Tim—like winter quarter of their freshman year, when they used to go for walks to Natural Bridges, hang out downtown, or get tea at Café Nightingale. She had been missing David and was lonely for intelligent company. She had been confused because of the whatever state they had left their relationship when they separated to go off to college—not officially broken up, but neither had they made a commitment to be faithful to each other. Somehow it just hadn't come up. Helen had wanted to discuss it, but it felt weird to just do it without any reason, and she could just imagine David's response: well, I'll probably be too busy to date, but if you want to, go ahead. As if she were some hopeless slut who couldn't survive a week without a guy.

Given their lack of a formal break-up, Helen had not felt entirely comfortable participating in the incessant scamming that was occurring all around her in Dorm I–but at the same time, she felt the need for companionship and physical fulfillment and wondered why she was denying herself the pleasure of that when for all she knew, David was breaking hearts left and right at Boston University. During that ambiguous period, Tim had been a safe harbor; masculine company that wouldn't threaten her relationship with David.

Helen had known Tim had a crush on her, but there was nothing she could do about it, other than gently guide him towards the notion of friendship, and transferring his romantic attentions to other women, of which there were more than a few who might have been receptive. She had encouraged him to show some interest in Lana, since she thought they might be good together (and Helen hated the way that Dorm II guy had used her for sex), but he seemed to resist. He seemed to be afraid of something; afraid of anything actually happening.

During spring quarter, when Tim had suddenly distanced himself from her and refused to hang out with them, Helen had wondered if she should just forget about him, but there were things that made her not write him off entirely, like his kindness towards her, and his insights into her life and their group of friends. He never tired of hearing stories about high school, and drew connections and parallels after hearing them, which always amazed Helen because they were so acute. He had an astonishing ability to predict what people would do. He seemed to want more out of life than just drinking beer and taking bong hits, and told her stories about making movies with his friend Shek back in Alta Lara, and how he wanted to be a screenwriter.

She and Tim had a bond that couldn't easily be broken. There was something she had with him that wasn't present in her crazed partying with the Alta Lara folks or Todd's friends from Dorm II. It was the same thing she felt with Jessica and Roxy, that closeness and security–what she hoped she would have felt with her siblings if she'd had brothers and sisters. With her group of friends in Alta Lara she had always felt like a newcomer, whose status was slightly lower than the rest–and a large part of her role in the group had come to be defined by her status as David's girlfriend.

Helen remembered when Tim had gradually re-emerged from his dark, skanky room on the first floor, near the end of that fateful spring quarter. He had hesitantly approached her after dinner. At first it was awkward, but gradually he started hanging out with them again. Tim had never really had a group of close friends before, so Helen was willing to cut him some slack. They never really talked about what had happened, since both were aware that Tim's desire for her had overwhelmed his urge to hang out with all of them. She had no solution to that–because there was none, just pain to be endured until it went away. Eventually, one day you would wake up and it would only hurt a little when you happened to think about it, instead of feeling completely overwhelming

In the end, their friendship had survived, just like it had survived the previous fall, when Tim had worked at that depraved movie theater and, apparently, lost his much-obsessed-over virginity to Joseph Harkes's daughter. Helen still wasn't sure if Tim's relationship with April had been a really good thing, or really bad. Tim needed that experience, but it had happened in such a bizarre way–trust Tim to be the kind of guy who needed a 7.1 earthquake to get laid–that it was hard to build on. If Tim had just been psyched that he had gotten the monkey off his back and moved on, he would have been okay. Unfortunately, it seemed like he'd gotten all of these absurdly romantic fantasies in his head. Helen remembered talking to him at a fall quarter party at Yalta Street, and Tim was going on about living with April while she went to art college and he to graduate school, like some kind of SNAGgy version of Humbert Humbert.

It had all seemed like a mad delusion to Helen. April was never going to be in a real relationship with Tim, given the different worlds they came from. She was a sixteen year old punk rock chick who had grown up too fast, hanging out with movie theater people, whom Helen knew from personal experience in Alta Lara, could be some of the most disreputable people around.

Helen wondered if she should have warned him off April the previous summer, when he had been coming to her for encouragement. At the time, she had been so happy he was showing enough interest in a girl to actually do something about it, that she had been willing to overlook the circumstances. Not that trying to dissuade Tim would have helped, anyway. Tim was determined to take his walk on the wild side, and so he had. For most of their friendship, Tim had not been judgmental of her, and she felt owed him the same. He had gotten enough shit from Jessica for the both of them, anyway.

All of these memories just made Helen miss Tim, and emphasized to her that he needed her too, that without her influence, and Jessica's, he seemed to go off the rails on a crazy train. She missed his sense of humor. She missed his insight. She missed having him in her life. He was one of those people that Helen needed to have her in her life–not all of the time, but a lot. He helped keep her sane.

♋

Twenty minutes later, Helen heard an irregular series of taps on her door, like someone trying to do a secret knock, and failing. Helen opened it and there stood Tim, wearing faded black jeans and a black turtleneck, and holding his backpack in front of him,. He shrugged, as if he expected Helen would be disappointed to see him, but he was going to force her to endure his company anyway. Helen's heart sank.

"Hi, Tim. Come in," she said, trying to sound more cheerful than she was.

"Hey." Tim entered and walked stiffly past her, darting his head around her house, appearing to study every detail, as if he were a detective at a murder scene as he headed straight for the kitchen. Helen shut her front door and followed.

When she joined him in the kitchen, Tim was standing in front of the table, opening his backpack and taking books out. Bristle, who had been curled up on the stack of newspapers next to the backdoor, got up when she saw Tim and started meowing. Tim instantly went over to Bristle, baby-talking to her as he did, in the same awful way Sophie talked to her cats at her parents' place in Napa.

"Meow meow, Bristle," Tim squawked. "Meow meow."

Helen went in the bathroom and peed. While she was seated on the toilet and waiting for the last drops to escape, she heard her front door open and close. Helen expected to hear Gretchen or Ellery say something, but heard nothing. Helen wiped, then got up to go to the bathroom and wash her face.

When she exited the bathroom, Bristle was in the living room, meowing plaintively. Tim was nowhere to be seen. Helen looked in the kitchen, and saw that his backpack still lay on the chair. Bristle followed her, still meowing and brushing against her legs. Helen stroked Bristle's back, feeling the sharp bumps of her shoulder blades and spine. Bristle meowed even louder, and started to hop up and down on her front legs.

"What's wrong, Bristle? Do you want to go outside?"

Helen opened the front door and felt the cool, fresh evening air waft lightly across her face and chest. She breathed in the sea-smelling air. Bristle, though, had no interest in going outside. Instead, she continued to meow and go in and out of Helen's legs.

"You silly girl," Helen said. She closed the door and returned to her seat. She wondered what had gotten into Tim. Maybe he had gone to get something from his car. She looked out the front window, at his blue Mazda still parked across the street. No sign of him anywhere. Was he ever going to get back to normal? He was acting like a mummy, the way Tim always did when he was depressed. He seemed to act it out, like he had decided he needed to be depressed and then performed the role to such an exaggerated degree that it was almost a joke, except that it wasn't. He wanted attention, but if you gave it to him, he pushed you away. As if whatever you thought he wanted, he wanted something else.

Reaching for *China Men*, Helen shoved Tim's scarecrow-like black-clad figure of gloom out of her mind and started to refresh her memory of the book. After a few minutes, Helen heard paw pads on the floor.

Bristle came in and looked up at Helen with her crossed, blue-white eyes, mewling and looking extremely retarded. She went over to her food dish. Helen saw the reason for her cat's distress—she was completely out of food. She remembered that she needed to buy cat food, which she had forgotten to do on her way home from school.

"I'm sorry, Bristle. I'll buy you some food, later. You can't be that hungry—you eat all the time."

After reading a few more pages, Helen heard her front door open and shut. Tim appeared, carrying a white and orange 7-Eleven bag. "I'm back," he said.

"Oh," Helen said, as neutrally as she could. "I didn't realize you were gone."

Helen returned her attention to *China Men*. She heard the sound of cat food being poured into a bowl. Bristle, meowing ecstatically, began devouring it. Tim placed the cat food box on the table between them, and sat.

"I got Bristle some food," he said.

"I see. Thanks."

"She seemed hungry."

"She eats too much," Helen said. "I just filled her food dish this morning. She needs to be put on a diet."

"Helen, that's ridiculous. She's so scrawny."

"She is not." Helen stared at him, challenging Tim to argue further. He looked back at her with a pseudo-superior expression, and opened an old-fashioned looking book with a pale blue cover in front of him.

"What are you reading?" he asked a moment later.

"*China Men.*"

"I remember that book. That's for Contemporary American Fiction, right?"

"Yeah. I'm re-reading it, or," Helen said with a regretful smile, "reading the stuff I skipped the first time."

"How do you like being a section leader, so far?"

"Oh, it's all right. It's too much work."

Helen paused. She felt restless. They were never going to get any work done here. They needed a change of scene. "Hey, do you want to go study at Claimstake?"

Tim looked at her, but said nothing. He looked to the side, then to the window they left open a crack to air the kitchen out. He let out his breath. Helen rolled her eyes at him. Did a simple trip to a 24-hour pancake house really present Tim with such a monumental decision? She bit her tongue and waited, forcing him to answer.

"Sure," he said slowly. "That would be fun. Just like last year... if not last summer," he added in a lower tone.

"Cool," Helen said. "I'll drive."

Helen gathered up her stuff and held the door open for Tim. As they walked down the staircase; Bristle shot past them, and then dodged left when she reached the bottom of the stairs, disappearing into the overgrown shrubbery.

One of the things Helen liked about Holly Street was that it was unusually wide for a side-street, which meant you didn't have to waste a lot of time parking neatly. Her sat in front of her house, two feet away from the curb and not strictly parallel with it, either. What could she say? She had been tired yesterday evening.

"Ah, the scarlet Volvo," Tim said to her car. "It's been a long time," he said, and patted it on the hood right in front of the passenger seat.

Helen noted that unlike his indifferent "hey" when he had first seen her, his greeting of both her cat and her car were far more affectionate and enthusiastic, as if the accessories of her life were more important to him than she was.

"It's red," Helen said, trying not to sound too exasperated.

"It's not red, it's scarlet," Tim said, as if it were the most obvious thing in the world. "Faded scarlet," he added, as if that would clear up any lingering confusion.

"It's red. Cars aren't scarlet."

"This one is," Tim said in an irritatingly complacent tone, as if God Himself had awarded him sole dominion over the naming of car colors. Helen wondered if Tim, in his overly literary way, was trying to draw some connection between her and that stupid book she had been forced to read in high school, *The Scarlet Letter*. If she ever found out that was truly the case, she promised herself she would kick his ass.

♋

Claimstake Pancakes was its usual quiet self when they arrived, looking exactly the same as it has the year before, and, Helen was sure, the same as it had every year since around 1970. The waitress, an older woman in a pink dress and white apron, just like Alice, seated them at one of the booths along the front wall. Helen sat facing the entrance, while Tim took the other side. As he sat, Helen saw his eyes darting all over the restaurant, as if there might be hidden gunmen sent to assassinate him hiding behind the counter and potted plants. Even for Tim, he seemed nervous and ill at ease, and he had never been the most comfortable person to begin with. Even once he was seated, he still kept looking around, as if he were looking for someone, or there someone looking for him that he didn't want to be seen by.

When the waitress brought them coffee, though, Tim stopped his nervous glancing long enough to tear open five packets of sugar and deposit them in his coffee. He gulped the resulting beige sludge, then took out his unbelievably battered blue binder from his backpack. Helen swore it must have been the same binder he had been using since his freshman year of high school. It had a faded black and yellow diamond 98.5 KRME sticker on the back, and beneath it, a Van Halen logo drawn in black ink. As Tim lifted it, Helen saw that only the smallest fragment of cardboard held the back cover on. She briefly fantasized about grabbing it from him and tearing the cover completely off to force him to get a new one, but decided not to. Instead, she took out *Las Mujeres de las Nubes* and looked with dread at the cover, a mosaic of three women created out of red, green and white triangles.

"What book is that?" Tim asked, grabbing for it like a greedy child reaching for some candy.

"Here, look," Helen said, handing to him before he could rip it out of her hands. He stared at the cover, and then opened it to the table of contents.

"The Women of the Clouds? The Men of the Iron Streets? The Children of the Rainbow?" he said, reading the names of the novel's three sections, his voice growing louder and more derisive with each one. "What the hell is this crap? Sounds like a bunch of Iron Maiden or Ronny James Dio songs."

As if to prove his point, Tim began singing in a strangulated howl, his attempt, she guessed, at mimicking the high-pitched wail of a heavy metal singer. "The children of the rainbow... escape the darkness below... run away, run away... Look out!" Tim's singing degenerated into a combination of laughter and coughing.

"I know, I know," Helen said, laughing, but also glancing around Claimstake to make sure no one she knew, or was even remotely associated with UCSZ, could hear them. The hostess in the pink dress and white shoes regarded them with skepticism, and Helen decided they'd better leave a sizeable tip. "I don't know why I took this class," Helen continued. "Jessica said she really liked it."

Tim turned the page and read for about thirty seconds with ferocious concentration, his brow growing more and more furrowed with each passing second. He closed the book with a snap.

"Wannabe Faulkner," he announced. "Lesbian Faulkner," he corrected himself.

"I don't think she's a lesbian, Tim."

"How do you know?"

"She has three children." The only part of the book Helen had been able to read was the author's profile on the inside back cover.

"Well, then she's a wannabe lesbian writing wannabe Faulkner. So UC Santa Zita. It's not really anything, just something that wants to be something else, written by someone who wants to be someone else. It's someone who wants to be something that they're not writing about something they don't know, in a style they're not talented enough to imitate," Tim concluded, and gasped for breath. His voice had been rising higher and higher during his diatribe until Helen was afraid he might burst a blood vessel.

"Can you tell me what it's about?" Helen asked while Tim was catching his breath, wondering if she could somehow steer his avalanche of derision in a useful direction.

"No idea," Tim said. "I think they're doing laundry. In a river. There are soldiers, but they can't see them. I think the women are actually ghosts, or something."

"Really?" Helen quickly scribbled down a note. "Tell me more."

Tim looked at her with the left corner of his mouth twitching downwards. "If I wanted to read something complicated, I would find something worthwhile, like *Tristram Shandy*. I don't even like real Faulkner that much. He's over-rated." Tim held up the book he was reading and shook it in front of Helen's face, as if she were at fault.

"You used to help me with my papers," she said.

"I used to do a lot of things," Tim replied in a voice lowered for dramatic affect, his eyes flicking back and forth like a rattlesnake's tongue.

"If you don't want to help me, then don't," Helen said.

Tim shrugged and resumed his nervous scanning of their surroundings. Helen decided that she might as well ask Tim now, before they got too deep into their work. Maybe it would even distract him from his constant surveillance.

"Hey, do you want to do something next Wednesday night?"

"Wednesday night? Ah," he said, and smiled archly. "Valentine's Day." Helen nodded. Tim was reacting just like she was afraid he was. "Just like last year," Tim said. "You don't have Todd to hang out with."

After a pause, Helen said, "So I guess you know we broke up?"

"Yeah, I know. Mick told me about it. He said you had. Broken up, I mean."

"Yes. Two weeks ago, now."

"Yeah," Tim said, and looked away. He fiddled with the papers in front of him.

"It's been really shitty," Helen said. "I'm taking it hard, I don't know why.

"Oh. Why has it been so hard?"

"I don't know." She did know, but she didn't know how to explain it without sounding sorry for herself.

"Well..." Tim let his breath out. "I guess that's good... that you finally decided it wasn't worth it."

"Actually, he broke up with me. He dumped me."

Tim looked up, eyes wide and focused on her. Helen was pleased to see that he was genuinely surprised by the revelation. "Oh. I didn't know." He seemed perplexed. Helen could almost see the gears whirring in his head. "Why?" he finally asked, in the most human tone he had used that entire night, seemingly baffled.

"Ask him," Helen said flatly. She let out her breath. She needed to talk about it. Who knows, Tim might even have something useful to say, like he used to. "No, I know why," Helen continued. "It was a lot of things. We weren't communicating any more. I think he knew it was basically over. He just wanted to be the one who ended it. If he hadn't, though, I would have."

"Good," Tim said, as if she were a recalcitrant child who had finally seen the error of her ways.

"What's that supposed to mean?" Helen asked. She scowled. She didn't need to be criticized, right now, especially by Tim.

"You and Todd never worked out, and he always ended up hurting you. It took you a year and a half to realize that." Tim's fingers shredded one of the used sugar packets on the table in front of him. "If I hadn't been around last year to console you, you probably would never have been able to stay with him as long as you did."

"That's not true," Helen said. "That's now how it works. I'm glad you were there for me when Todd and I were broken up, but I could still deal."

"Really? Tim said, and shook his head as if he didn't believe Helen was a reliable authority on the subject. "So... then how does it work? Tell me."

"Talking to you might have helped me, but it wasn't all or nothing. It's all... mixed up... You wouldn't understand," Helen finally said, infuriated by Tim's impassive mien, like a cruel teacher enjoying the humiliation of a student who'd been called on and didn't know the answer.

"Why?"

"You know why..." Helen smiled maliciously. Tim was going to get what he had coming to him. "You're not exactly an expert on real relationships."

Tim, who had been bending forward, boring his eyes on her, sat back and looked away. He looked to his right, down the line of booths to the circular one in the corner. He fiddled with the ceramic sugar packet holder.

"Maybe I am," he said in a quieter voice. "Only in a different way. I have an objective viewpoint."

As if Tim were an independent observer sent by aliens to study her. His tendency to think of himself as a watcher and not a participant in life maddened her.

"Give me a break," Helen said. "I stayed with Todd for my own reasons and it's my business," she said flatly, no longer interested in Tim's opinions.

Tim made a triangle out of his hands, touching his fingertips together. "Okay, okay. But now you're single. Maybe you'll be happier that way."

"Maybe. I want to start dating again," Helen said, surprising herself, since the words just seemed to pop out of their own volition, and she wasn't sure she actually agreed with them.

"So soon?" Tim asked, seeming crestfallen at the news.

"Why not?"

"I don't know. Why are you in such a hurry?"

"I'm not, I just want to go on a date, that's all. And meet new people. Get out the rut."

"Yeah, I'd like to do that, too. But I don't think I can. It wouldn't be a good idea. I need to figure out some stuff in my life, before I start really living it again."

As if living one's life were optional—just something you only had to do when you felt like it. Well, if you had a trust fund, and were as smart as Tim, maybe that was true. "Okay, Helen said. Call me when you do."

She looked down at *China Men*. She had to keep reading, find interesting things she could say tomorrow, to fill the gaps in conversation before Peak took over.

But it was no use. She felt Tim's hurt, glowering presence across the table. Any mention by her of his lack of romantic experience, no matter how true or deserved, inevitably made him retreat into this sullen shell. She shouldn't have brought that up—but his comment that it was only because of him that she was able to stay with Todd had really irritated her. She closed the paperback with an emphatic slap.

"Look, I'm sorry," she said, once he looked up.

Behind his over-sized spectacles, Tim blinked furiously. He regarded her with trepidation. "It's okay, it's okay," he said quickly. "I'm sorry, too. Very sorry."

"About?"

"You and Todd. You guys. Everything," he said, and shrugged. "I'm sorry about everything," he said, in a quiet tone that sounded like the last words of a dying man.

"What is up with you?" she asked. "Is there something bothering you? Like specifically?" Helen asked.

For only the second time since they had gotten to Claimstake, Tim looked her straight in the eye, his small brown pupils boring in on her through the warped curvature of his glasses.

"Being here," Tim said. "It's weird. I used to come here with April. It reminds me of her, that's all. We came here a few times–her, August, Caleb–that whole group. Last summer," Tim said, after another ridiculously long pause. "The summer of '89," he said, as if it was a movie or a Bryan Adams song–a distant, long ago time that could only be seen through the sepia tinge of nostalgia.

"Was the summer of '89 really all that great?" Helen asked. She remembered fighting with Todd, fighting with David, shitty jobs, having no money, too many men in her bed. "Anyway, if you miss them, so much, why don't you still hang out with them?"

"I've been cast out," Tim said, then got a faraway look in his eyes peering through the windows, into the misty night. Helen looked at their reflections in the high glass window that extended from table level to the ceiling, studying Tim's gaunt visage superimposed on the view of Marr Street, his face's reflection superimposed on a motel with a flashing red VACANCY sign. He could be maddeningly vague sometimes, like he wanted someone to have to make a big effort to get what he was saying out of him. Sometimes Helen was willing to play that game, but not tonight. Her life was hard enough right now without someone else intentionally making it harder.

"Please," Helen said.

"I know, I know," Tim said. "Too many Kane College cardiac injuries," he said bitterly.

"I'm sorry about that, Tim," Helen said quietly. "I know you really liked that girl."

"Girls," Tim said.

"Couldn't you just pick one?" Helen asked.

"I thought I had," Tim said. "But I lost them both. Or all three. Not that I ever really had a chance with any of them."

During Tim's previous sentences, his voice had grown so quiet it was as if he was just talking to himself. Helen hated that feeling, like she was just a prop in Tim's imagination, and that he could have just as well been holding the conversation in his mind.

"I don't think you and April ever had a future," Helen said. "I don't know about the others."

Tim nodded, a barely perceptible movement of his chin. "I know. But for a while, it seemed like maybe we did. And I didn't go for Robin, the way I should have. So now I'm being punished. We're all being punished."

"No, we're not," Helen said, with asperity. Tim's words were like a personification of the self-pity she heard in herself and was trying to get away from.

Tim shrugged. He didn't argue with her, but Helen knew he still felt that way. Both looked at each other, as if the other should say something, but neither did. Finally, they both looked down and resumed reading.

☞

The rest of their time at Claimstake passed quietly. Helen actually managed to finish grading her papers, which was a major relief. She saw Tim maniacally scribbling little notes in the margins of his book, so she guessed Tim's night was a success, as well, at least academically. They paid the bill, left a 25% tip and exited the restaurant.

Helen knew she should ask him about Valentine's Day again. She hoped her apology would smooth things over enough that Tim would be willing to hang out; if that indeed was what was standing in the way of them being friends again. Otherwise, she didn't know what she was going to do–she was starting to feel abandoned by everyone who professed to care about her.

She opened Tim's door for him, then circled around the back of her car and got in the driver's seat. Once she had pulled out of the parking lot and onto Marr Street, she broached the topic again.

"So, did you want to do something on Wednesday?" Helen asked.

"Mmm... I might be busy," Tim said.

"Doing what?" Helen asked, and it came out sounding half-angry, half-desperate. Despite herself, she felt her eyes moistening at this absurd rejection. She needed someone to give a shit about her right now.

"I'm sorry," Tim burbled. "I mean I guess I could do something."

"It's okay. It's not like I don't have work to do, too," Helen said. She felt her face redden with shame and embarrassment. She vision temporarily blurred, she nearly drove through a stop sign after she crossed the river. Her car shuddered to a halt with the brakes screeching like the suffering of the damned.

Tim said nothing. Despite his tendency to be critical, Tim never said anything bad about her driving, for which she was grateful. It was one of the many small things about Tim that added up to why he had become one of her closest friends. Helen wiped her eyes, and then glanced to her right. To her surprise, he was looking at her with concern, almost tenderness–as if for the first time that evening, really seeing her.

"Sorry," he said again. "We can hang out."

Helen's Volvo approached the San Cristobal River. The Frampton Street Bridge arced over it. The pause in their conversation grew–not awkward, but definitely not natural either. Helen switched the radio on to her favorite station, KTNT. She preferred that station to KRME, the one they had all listened to in high school, because they sometimes played cheezy songs from the 70s, ones that reminded her of riding in the car with her mom, like "Dream Weaver" and "Spinning Wheel."

At this moment, though, KTNT let her down and was playing something that Helen didn't recognize but sounded lame. Tim, though, seemed to be very excited by it, and sat up straighter. "Sweet," he exclaimed, and started singing along with it in his off-key way.

"That's a terrible song," Helen said.

"Come on, it's the new Robert Plant," Tim said. "It rocks."

"Please," Helen said. "He's like fifty years old. He should be gardening, or bee-keeping."

Much to Helen's relief, the song quickly faded. The road in front of them sloped upwards as it ascended the bridge across the San Cristobal, lined by dull orange lights on both sides. A single pedestrian trudged upwards, hands in both his pockets, alone.

It only took Helen a second to recognize the next song, though. The guitar riff was so distinctive, a single chord that only came out of the driver side speakers. Helen couldn't remember the song's name, of course, but it didn't matter, because she was sure Tim did. Anyway, she knew all the words. Helen and Tim smiled at each other. Tim rolled down his window and Helen turned up the volume.

"Those crazy nights," Tim and Helen both sang lustily, perfectly on cue with the singer, if not exactly in key.

Helen's Volvo sped up the incline, past the single pedestrian and they briefly had a view of downtown Santa Zita. The gaping holes in the line of rooftops where the buildings had been torn down gave it an unnaturally uneven appearance, like a boxer smiling after a fight where he had lost half his teeth.

For the next few minutes, Helen and Tim sang along with the song, and with each other. As they sped along the river, Tim alternated between playing air guitar and air drums so frenetically Helen thought he might snap his seatbelt or break the windshield. They passed the movie theater where Tim had engaged in so much disreputability, but he was so transported by the song he didn't seem to have time to engage in any more obsessive nostalgia.

"That totally reminds me of freshman year," Tim said. "Do you remember? When we drove to Terra Nueva and got totally lost, pounded a six-pack in that parking lot?"

"Totally," Helen said. "Totally."

"You dared me to pimp for alcohol, and I did! Only time ever," Tim said, shaking his head in remembrance.

The song began to fade out, as Tim finger wiggled on an invisible fret-board and Helen raced through a yellow light that turned red the second after she decided they could make it. As they zoomed through, Helen glanced right and left to make sure no cops had seen her.

A right turn onto Redwood, then a left onto Holly just in front of a Santa Zita County Transit bus. Helen roared down Holly Street, parking just as the guitar solo faded out. With a satisfying click, Helen switched her car off. Tim bounced out of the car and stretched out his arms.

"That felt good," he said.

Helen and Tim said good night, and Helen was pleased to see Tim reaching out to give her a quick hug. "You'll call me about Wednesday night?" Helen asked.

"Yeah, totally," Tim said, and rushed across the street to his blue Mazda. Helen waited on the sidewalk until the Mazda started and sped away towards Redwood.

Helen smiled to herself. Listening to that song was the most alive she's felt in weeks. Kind of sad that it took a Journey song to make her feel inspired. Worse, a Journey song from high school. What was her life coming to?

As she stood on the sidewalk, she heard some piteous mewling. Bristle appeared from underneath a parked car and brushed herself against Helen's legs.

"Oh, Bristle," Helen said, half-worried, half exasperated. She reached down and scooped up her little cat with one hand. Bristle instantly started purring, and rubbing her head against Helen's cheek, but at the same time struggling to get away. Helen held her cat for a few more moments, but finally the clawing started hurting more than she was enjoying the affection.

"Okay, okay," Helen said. "Here you go." She loosened her grip on Bristle, and her cat sprang from her body, scratching her on the arm in the process. Bristle hit the ground and bounded up the stairs without missing a beat.

Helen followed her. She took the rest of the food Tim had bought and poured it into Bristle's bowl. Why was her cat so crazy? Helen wondered if the experience of living at Holly Street had permanently wounded Bristle, rendered her unable to interact with human beings normally. What age was Bristle in human years? She was past puberty, of course. She had already been fixed, thanks to the SPCA. Were she and Bristle the same age, allowing for the conversion of human to kitty years? Was Bristle's need to venture outside, get dusty and collect fleas somehow the feline equivalent of going away to college?

She looked into Bristle's goofily skewed pale blue eyes, but her cat had no answer, other than to broadcast a new sequence of increasingly desperate meows. Helen looked at the clock and saw it was time for bed. At least she had all of her papers evaluated now. She would be spared her students pestering her about when their papers would be done.

Four

Only by locking her jaw and staring at the Dead Kennedys logo carved in the tabletop, the only piece of graffiti legible from where she was standing, could Helen prevent the yawn from escaping her mouth. Hadn't Jello Biafra gone to UCSZ? Maybe he had inscribed it there personally.

Her mouth hurt because she was clenching it so hard. The classroom was terribly hot and crowded. A ring of students filled every seat at the four tables arranged in a square, and around them gathered still more, standing or sitting against the walls of the room. The multitude of bodies made the room seem far smaller than it was. Flies buzzed against the windows and occasionally flew around the people in the outer circle before they were shooed away.

As always, most of the section seemed lost in half-attention, looking out the window at the bright corn-flower blue winter sky, doodling in their notebooks, or even catching up on their reading. Helen wished she hadn't done all those things so many times in UCSZ classes so she could feel more justified in her irritation. She glanced around and took stock of her students one by one. Helen had never really realized, from a teacher's perspective, just how pathetically obvious it was who was paying attention, and who wasn't. As a student, she had always felt like part of an anonymous, undifferentiated mass, but now she knew that her teachers and professors must have taken note of her boredom all these years. You had to have a pretty thick skin to be a teacher–thicker than what Helen wore. She just wished someone, anyone, would say something. Someone other than Peak.

As usual, Peak's voice filled the room, seeming to drown out not only the possibility of others' speaking, but thinking as well. His words were delivered with such confidence–such overwhelming conviction that the world needed to hear them, and with such complete disregard and awareness of the tedium and torpor they induced in those unlucky enough to still be paying attention–that it infuriated Helen, but she had no conception of how to convince him to shut up that wouldn't make the class think she was on some kind of power trip.

Besides Peak, the other member of the section likely to be paying attention at any given moment was Michael Sullivan, a freshman who looked younger than that, like he had just wandered into the section from a local high school; though possibly not a high school in this decade. Helen could feel Michael's eyes on her most of the time, though he rarely spoke. She had tried making eye contact with him a few times just for the hell of it, but he was too shy and always looked down, pretending to be absorbed in writing his notes. Michael took by far the most notes in the class. It showed in his papers, which were detailed and well-written, though a little dry. She thought of trying to draw him out somehow, but all she could think of was to call on him, since he never opened his mouth voluntarily, and just the thought of turning that power-mad gave her the creeps. She wondered, too, if, there was something more than just scholarly interest in his gaze. She got that vibe, and usually when she felt something like, it turned out be real. Especially when she didn't want it to be.

"It's like last summer when I was back-packing in Guatemala," Peak was going on. "You would go to these villages with, like, no TV or radio, and it was like, man, you really don't need that stuff."

Peak brought up his trip to Central America during fall quarter at least once a section. Of all the indignities the United States had inflicted on Central America, she thought that three months of Peak might have been the worst. Helen glanced around the room, to gauge her section's interest in the latest volume of the "Life & Travels of Peak, UC Santa Zita Student At Large."

Helen's eyes finally landed on Maria Gaier, who sat directly across from her position at the center of the table parallel with the chalkboard. As usual, Maria wore a disdainful look, the same one she wore during most of the conversations in their section. She wore a simple cotton print dress, which seemed in a curious way to emphasize her advantage in both age and height over Helen. Compared to her, Helen felt like a high schooler in her blue sweater, white jeans, and sneakers.

Maria was a fifth-year senior taking the class because it was the only she could get into which satisfied her major requirements, a complicated story involving a double women's studies/literature major and a planned quarter abroad at the Sorbonne. Helen knew this because she had talked to Maria after the first section meeting. Helen had been impressed by some of her comments in the first section, and thought it a good idea to cultivate her acquaintance, since she might be a useful ally.

As the quarter had gone on, though, Helen's opinion of Maria had, like her opinion of so many of her students, only worsened. Maria's attitude was patronizing, and Helen got the feeling that only her profound sense of sisterhood prevented Maria from letting Helen just how lame a section leader she really was. Also, she had stopped being a good contributor, as if the quality of discourse in the section was not up to a high enough standard for her to take part in. Such arrogance drove Helen crazy. Especially from a woman; and a woman who claimed allegiance to the feminist cause.

Their eyes met for a second, and Helen hoped that it would challenge Maria to break into Peak's monologue. But no such luck. Instead, Maria just averted her eyes to the window facing the Terra Nueva Bay.

"So I was like talking to this guy who was some kind of, like, tour guide, or shaman, or whatever, and he was telling me about climbing the volcano at night, and I was like 'yeah, okay, cool, I'll do that.' But then he totally flaked, so I just went off into the jungle by myself. I saw a tarantula, which was intense, because that's my like, totem animal. One of them, anyway."

"Thank you, Peak," Helen said.

"No prob," he said. Helen could tell he had only been pausing to take a breath, gathering himself to launch into the next chapter of the saga, in which he ended up falling asleep in a clearing (baked out of his gourd, Helen was sure) and waking up covered with stinging red ants. Just imagining Peak being stung half to death was almost worth listening the story, but not quite. He gave her a winning smile, as if were granting her a huge favor by letting her break in.

Helen picked up the chalk and, instead of answering the question of whether it was possible to kill someone with a piece of chalk by flinging it at Peak's huge dome of dark curly hair, turned to the blackboard. Peak's tale had made her think about geography, and the paper she had written for the class that had gotten her into this mess in the first place, so she wrote China and USA and underlined both. "These are the two worlds of *China Men*."

"What about Hawaii?" one student asked from the corner between the two windowed walls.

"That's part of the US," Helen said, but then reconsidered.

"I think it's like where the two worlds collide," another girl said, while Helen was gathering her thoughts.

Helen nodded, amazed that actual intellectual discourse seemed to be occurring in her section. "That's great, Jennifer."

As Jennifer continued on, Helen wrote Hawaii on the blackboard between the USA and China, drew a wiggly circle around it in a vague attempt to replicate what she remembered Hawaii looking like on a map. She had only been there once, and it hadn't been for vacation. She and her mother had spent two hours in Honolulu, changing flights. It had been the first stop on the journey that had taken them from Guam to Minnesota, to begin their new, husband and father-less life. She remembered how sweet the air had smelled, like a bouquet of flowers, instead of a wet blanket of rotting lettuce as it had in Guam. She and her mother had stopped there to transfer between the military transport from Guam and the United flight that would take them to LA. After that they would connect to Minneapolis, their final destination on the far side of the world.

Helen and her mother had ridden the *wiki–wiki* bus between terminals, since the bus from the Air Force base had dropped them off at the wrong one. Unlike the Air Force bases, where people were constantly telling you where to go and what to do, in the civilian world you were pretty much left to figure it out for yourself. Helen's mother had tried to cheer her up by pointing out the silly, sing-song name of the bus. But Helen had been too scared, and too determined to be grown-up and not show she was afraid, to enjoy the name and had just scowled, said "yeah, that's so cute, mom." Her mother's face had fallen and her eyes started to water.

In that moment, Helen had felt a chasm open between them and the rest of the world. They were surrounded by fat and happy tourists talking and laughing excitedly about the week in paradise they were about to enjoy. Helen had hated them all and wanted to shout "can't you see my mom is sad?!" She hated their huge butts in shorts big enough to be used as tents, plastic flower leis and Polaroid instant cameras around their neck. She especially hated the children; crying because they hadn't been bought a present in the airport gift shop, not because their parents had just split up, and their mother had told them they would never see their father again, and not only that, she should never want to, and even if she did it wouldn't be allowed, and she might be slapped just for asking; and they were going to Minnesota where it snowed in the winter and if you got locked out of your house you would die from the cold.

Helen had wanted so badly to stay longer in Honolulu, to see the stuff she had seen on TV–the beaches, surfing, and volcanoes. She wanted to see *Hawaii 5-0*. But they had no time, her mother said, not enough money to stay even one night. Maybe another time. A few years later, when they had moved to Alta Lara and their financial situation had somewhat improved, her mother had talked about it, but they always ended up going somewhere else. Meanwhile, Sarah went there seemingly at the drop of a hat since her family had a timeshare in a condo on Maui. Jake and Todd Forrest had gone during senior year. Helen was invited but had to decline, since she had to save her money for her freshman year at UCSZ.

Helen forced herself to stop ruminating, aware that Jennifer had finished. "But what does Hawaii really mean as a place?" Helen asked. "Isn't it kind of a stop, on the way to someplace else?"

"Not for the people who lived there, before the white man came and killed them all," said the short-haired girl. "Hawaii was their home," she added plaintively.

Everyone in the section nodded and murmured in agreement. Helen had the distinct feeling that they all felt she had made a terrible faux pas.

"Well," Helen said, "that's true, Brianne."

"It's Brionne," the girl said.

"Sorry," Helen said, to which Helen added "stupid little valley girl PC-wannabe bitch" in her mind. Now, instead of her jaw, her teeth were starting to hurt from gritting them so much.

The pause that followed was so awkward it seemed to suck every possible idea out of Helen's brain. She waited for Peak to fill it with one of his idiot monologues, but he seemed to have fallen inexplicably silent. She glanced at him, and he was apparently so absorbed in his next masterpiece of doodling that he couldn't be bothered to participate. Helen licked her lips and suddenly realized what it means to have stage fright. Someone coughed and paper rustled. All Helen could think of was the scene on that bus and how impossibly lost she had felt, and after that, how terrifyingly dark the flight had seemed. She had tried to sleep, but instead she just stared out the oval window at the black sky, infinite darkness above and below, no moon, no stars, no anything; nothing but a black void that had seemed to swallow Helen, her mother, and everyone else on the plane. It had been such a relief when she had dozed off, then came awake to see bands of red, pink and yellow light in the east—reassurance that the world hadn't come to an end after all.

Movement, unexpected movement, that Helen would have thought was a student raising their hand if it hadn't come from a table with some of her most somnolent students, caught Helen's eye. She thought at first it was just a fly being swatted away, but then she saw it was one of the freshmen, Michael, slowly raising his hand, and looking as if he would take it back down at the slightest opportunity. Helen didn't intend to give him that chance.

"Michael, right?" She smiled at him.

"But they came from other parts of Polynesia," Michael said. "The Hawaiian islands were only settled for a few hundred years before Captain Cook d– sailed there."

"Thank you, Michael," Helen said with relief. "That's a good point."

Michael smiled shyly, the first time Helen could remember him smiling. That smile disappeared the second Peak's voice came booming across the room. "But those people were peaceful, man. They didn't even have, like, weapons."

A few of the other students murmured in agreement. Helen saw Michael frown in disbelief. It seemed like he was about to say something, but held back. Helen had no idea who was right, and she didn't think there was much point to getting in an argument about history, which she could just see going round and round in circles with no resolution. Instead, she tried to bring the conversation back to the book.

"What about the women?" Helen asked. "Where are they happiest?"

Helen stood with her back to the chalkboard, satisfied that for at least once her section was having a half-way decent discussion. The subject had shifted from *China Men* to Raymond Carver, whom they had already covered the week before, but that was fine with Helen as long as they didn't have to hear more about Peak's escapades in Guatemala.

Apparently the quality of discussion had reached Maria's minimum standard, because she was actually paying attention. She raised a finger and Helen gestured that she should speak.

"I think the impulse to fix the meaning of texts in an absolute way is part of a patriarchal system which freezes literary interpretation in order to prevent feminist re-readings," Maria said.

Helen forced her eyes upwards. She saw that her section, by their expressions, postures and murmurs of assent, agreed with Maria. She was torn between pleasure that Maria had broken her contemptuous silence, and irritation at the flat, authoritative tone the words were delivered in. Feeling that Maria was being way more dogmatic than was appropriate, Helen decided to try and open the conversation up.

"What do other people think? Is it a good idea if there is one true meaning to a book, or story, or whatever?"

"I think ultimately there must be a truth in what we read, else the act of reading would be pointless—an endless circle of people interpreting and re-interpreting, with no end, ever," Michael said. He looked at her as he was speaking, as if for comfort, or approval.

"Maybe that's what it is, man," said one student, who had a brown pony-tail and wore and orange and green pullover. He gained an appreciative laugh from many of the other students in the section, which he received with a grin and a self-conscious smoothing of some hairs that had escaped the rubber-band holding the rest.

"But if that's so," said Michael, "how can literature ever actually do something? Like educate, or..."

Several students nodded in agreement. "That's true," one murmured. "Good point," another said.

Helen nodded as well. She liked the sound of Michael's well-phrased words. His measured and reasonable tones distracted her from the caffeine jitters she'd been feeling all day. She hoped someone other than Maria would respond, but then she saw Maria lift her pinky finger, a motion that made her seem weirdly aristocratic.

"I'm not sure that's what education should be," said Maria.

Helen looked around the room. She was pleasantly surprised to see that most of the students were paying attention, but none of them added anything. They merely followed the conversation between Michael and Maria by turning their heads back and forth. Helen found Michael very appealing because she knew he was being absolutely honest–which was rare in her section, or at UCSZ in general. He wasn't trying to please anyone with what he said. She hoped it didn't get him in trouble. She was about to say something, to unite the two sides harmoniously, because she thought it was silly for people to disagree about something like literature, when Peak raised his hand slightly.

"It's all true, though," Peak said. "Everyone has their own truth, you know. It's capitalist bullshit to say there's just one way to do something. The government wants you to think there's only one truth. But you have to break on through that. To the other side," he concluded with a crooked smile.

Again the students sitting at the table nodded and murmured agreement. Michael, though, frowned and blurted out, "But you have to be careful about the truth, and make sure you have the right one. I think Carver was demonstrating the degree to which everyone is intellectually responsible for his or her own salvation or damnation."

Helen's eyes widened. She knew Michael's statement would get a negative reaction. What's more, she knew that he wouldn't expect such a personal response in an intellectual discussion. She felt hot in her face and the lower middle of her chest, hearing the rustle of bodies as the students tried to release the accumulated tension. Maria Gatellis rolled her eyes at Michael's statement. Helen heard murmurs and giggles and a whispered mockery, aimed against this obvious freshman that had violated the unwritten laws of the UCSZ section.

Maria looked into Helen's eyes, narrowing her eyes slightly. Helen felt a little intimidated by her direct gaze, but she could not allow the upper-class-woman to usurp her position. Helen decided to deflect Maria, and the rest of the section who had set themselves firmly against Michael, by stating their judgment in a more gentle way.

"Well, Michael, I think you're right to a degree. But you know, there are many things beyond the characters' control. To place all the blame on the individual removes any responsibility from society."

Maria stared hard at Helen. Helen looked back with what she hoped was a pleasantly neutral expression. She wiped her hand on her pants. Her hand felt sweaty and scummy because of all the coffee she had drunk, and the ache in her left temple was getting harder to ignore. She remembered as she was wiping her hand that she had worn her white jeans that day, and realized with annoyance that there was now a faint brown stain on her leg. She leveled her head and smiled to her section as a whole, hoping the crisis had passed. But Peak had more to say, and with great misgivings, Helen gestured for him to speak.

"I think that saying someone's responsible for everything that happens to them is just a way of blaming the victim," Peak said. "Here we have people getting totally screwed over by the system, and then you're saying it's they're fault? I think that's way out of line, dude."

Helen stood and watched this exchange, trying to think of a way to steer her section away from the argument, since no good was going to come of further discussion. She looked at the faces of the students and sighed inwardly. They seemed set on judgment.

"But the question isn't society, the question is the individual's response to society," Michael responded, his voice breaking at the end.

Nobody said anything. It was as if Michael had ceased to exist. He slumped, and seemed, to Helen, to withdraw from the world. Helen shrugged, and decided it was time to move on. Forgetting again, she wiped her hand again on her pants several times. She looked across the room to Michael. For the first time, his eyes met hers unyieldingly, but they were sad and disappointed. She had let him down. She realized just how much he liked her, and the absurdity of it all almost made her break out in laughter in front of the entire section. It was all so ridiculous. Why? Why not? What was wrong with him? Not only did he have no idea how to act in a UCSZ section, what business did he have getting a crush on her?

Helen felt helpless to aid Michael, and angry at him for being so defenseless and making an ass of himself. He was smart enough, but he lacked the social skills; the sense, the knowledge of what to say (and more importantly what not to say) in a UCSZ section.

Helen broke her gaze away and did not look back in Michael's direction for the rest of the section. There were only about five minutes left, so Helen decided to wrap things up. She told her class, "I have your papers from two weeks ago."

Helen passed out the evaluated papers to her students, noting that none of them would make eye contact with her. When she gave out the last one, she almost ran out of the room, she was so glad the section was over. Thank God she had coffee with Roxy at Fremont College to look forward to. Without that, she thought she might just go lie down in a bed of ferns under the redwoods and do nothing until the sun went down and the moon rose.

♋

Helen rushed up to Roxy, who stood just outside the coffee shop doors and smiled widely when she saw Helen hurrying down the hall. She and Helen hugged, then went inside and stood in line. "How was section?" Roxy asked.

Unwilling to face the reality of what had just transpired, Helen chose something ridiculous to focus on, in the hopes that Roxy might find it amusing. "Oh, God. One of the freshmen has a crush on me."

"No way."

"I know. It's so bothersome."

"Is he cute?"

"No, not really. He's kind of underdeveloped, physically."

"A nerd?"

"Sort of. Really serious. He never smiles."

"Weird."

"Yeah." Out of the corner of her eye, Helen spied someone from her section enter the coffee shop–a sophomore guy named Matt. Vaguely cute, but a little too short. She looked away, hoping he hadn't seen her. She shivered and yawned simultaneously. She saw the girl in front of her buy a tall, steaming cup of coffee. It looked too good to pass up. Helen knew she shouldn't drink more coffee, but she didn't know how she was going to get through the rest of the day without it.

Once Roxy and Helen both bought coffee, Helen led her friend to a small table in the corner, vacated just as they left the counter. "I'm sorry about Tuesday night," said Helen as they sat.

"You don't have to be sorry about anything. You needed to really talk about it."

"I feel so ridiculous. It's been two weeks. You'd think I'd get over it."

"Don't worry about it. Some things take time." Roxy said, and grabbed Helen's hand. Helen felt her slender fingers squeeze. She wished she had hands as elegant as Roxy's. Hers were more stubby and mannish.

"Thanks, Roxy. I just feel so stupid."

"You need to forget about it and move on."

"Yeah."

"Any hot prospects?" asked Roxy. "Other than the freshman."

Helen mock pouted, and said, "No."

"I would think being a TA would help."

"Not in a lit class. The only good looking guys in literature sections are gay. Or incurably annoying."

"Can I quote you on that?"

"Sure." Helen gulped her coffee. She remembered Michael again. She should have been nicer to him. She should have stopped her section from coming down so hard on him. He didn't know any better.

During the pause, Roxy had been looking outside. She looked back at Helen, and let her breath out. "You know, I've been thinking, relationships don't seem to ever work out in Santa Zita. Look at Peter and Jamie—"

"Or you and Torrance."

"Yeah. And you haven't had any better luck, either. Granted, you were with Todd for a long time, but it was very up and down."

"To say the least," Helen agreed. "Mostly down."

"It's like the whole place is cursed."

"Everyone here just has a stick up their butt, that's all."

"I don't know. It's like the coolest people are the ones who have the most trouble."

Helen moved her hair out of her eyes and said, "Maybe." There was probably more to it than that. But Helen didn't feel like pursuing it any further. She didn't want to think about

Todd, and even if Roxy wanted to talk about Torrance, Helen didn't really want to think about him, either. She had gotten rid of Todd–why couldn't Roxy forget about Torrance, and, for that matter, why didn't Gretchen break up with Bill? Didn't they see how stupid it was to be obsessed with guys that were such dicks?

"What's wrong?" Roxy asked.

"Nothing," Helen said. "Why do you ask?"

"You look kind of irritated."

"Oh, I'm just PMSing. Or it's too much coffee. I don't know."

Both were silent for a minute. Helen felt a sudden desire to leave the cafe, but she before she could take her leave, Roxy had thought of something else. "Here's some gossip–Jake has a date."

"Really?" Helen said.

Over winter break Jake had broken up again with his girlfriend from Alta Lara, Christa. Helen hadn't actually been that bummed, since she thought Christa was a possessive bitch. Helen had been friends with Jake for a long time, and though she thought he was, objectively speaking, attractive, she had never really been psyched on him, and her manner towards him indicated that. They flirted, but it was the kind of flirtation that was obviously, to anyone with an ounce of perception, never meant to go anywhere. Christa's attitude towards her, then, was an indication to Helen that she was pathologically insecure–an opinion that was echoed by Jake's other female friends from Alta Lara, like Sarah and Alice.

"With who?" Helen asked.

"Some chick he met in his French class."

"Ah, *oui*," Helen said. She smiled, but at the same time she felt a little pang. Jake had broken up with his girlfriend, but now he had a date. Life went on, at least for him.

"I should go," Helen said. "What's up for this weekend?"

"Nada," Roxy replied. "That I know of. I might have to study", she said, and grimaced.

"God," Helen said. "What's happening to us? Are we getting old?" Roxy shrugged. "Let's go see a movie," Helen said. "Study break."

"Sure." Roxy replied. "Any one in particular?"

"*Crazy For Love*," Helen said, and embellished the title with a wild movement of her eyes, eyebrows and cheekbones. She had seen an ad for it while riding the bus up to campus earlier that day, reminding her it was opening on Friday. She loved the directors' previous film, *Mister Lonely*, and there were worse ways to spend two hours than looking at some filet like Nicolas Cage.

"Sure," Roxy laughed. "Call me when."

"Okay. Maybe I'll call Tim," Helen said. She remembered him talking about the movie last fall–as usual, he had known about it before anyone else.

"I haven't seen him all quarter. Since Peter's birthday party." Roxy said. A slight inclination of her head indicated to Helen that she knew about their estrangement. Helen wondered who had told her about it–probably Jessica.

"Neither have I," Helen said simply. "But we hung out last night."

"He feeling any better?"

"I guess... yeah. It was okay. We're supposed to hang out again this Wednesday."

"Isn't that Valentine's Day?"

"Yes," Helen said, and paused for a perfectly calibrated amount of time meant to speak volumes. "It is. My least favorite day of the year."

"Valentine's Day sucks."

"Yeah it does. So I'm boycotting it."

"Good for you. Is Tim?"

Helen gave Roxy a sharp look. "Who knows?" Helen said. "I think he's still pining away for that high school chick from last summer."

"Are you kidding?"" Roxy said incredulously. "The one Torrance sold weed to?" She shook her head and rolled her eyes.

"Whatever on that," Helen said. "I really need to go."

"Alright. See you this weekend. Adios."

Roxy bent down, and gave Helen a hug. They exited the cafe, Roxy going through the back sliding glass doors that led in the direction of Humphrey College, while Helen went out the front doors towards the Fremont courtyard. As she walked along the terraced courtyard, she took in the view of the Terra Nueva Bay and Peninsula, magnificent as always, luring her with its seeming independence from the rest of the land. She briefly fantasized about moving there, getting a high-paying waitress job at a swanky restaurant, and being able to afford her own place. She would still be close enough that she could keep in touch with Jessica, Roxy and her other friends, but it would still qualify as a new life.

Five

Making a conscious effort not to jam too hard, Helen jiggled the key in the lock, She waited for it to catch, and once it did, shoved the door open. The house was dark, which meant her housemates weren't home, which was a relief. Out of habit, she glanced at the answering machine. The red light blinked ominously, like the eye of a dragon lurking in a cave. She had no intention of listening to the messages. Not today, when she was too tired, too stressed. Even as she stood, caught between the answering machine and the corner of the wall, thoughts of what those messages might be clicked in her mind. Her mother, wondering why she hadn't called. Sarah, wondering the same. A student, wondering where their paper was. Joseph Harkes, demanding yet another meeting. The credit card company, wondering where their money was.

As the potential disasters that the blinking light might portend cascaded through her mind, Helen realized she was still standing, holding her backpack, paralyzed. The thoughts kept flashing by despite her efforts to cut them off. With a chilling stab in her stomach, she wondered if she might be losing control of her mind. She threw her backpack on the couch and went in her room. She moved the pile of laundry she was planning to do that weekend off the bed. She fell on to her bed and had just enough energy left to kick off her shoes. They hit the door with a satisfying clunk.

Helen drifted off into a troubled half-sleep. Every time she was about to completely lose consciousness, the phone would jangle her awake. After four rings separated by an endless wait, the answering machine clicked on. The messages all sounded like they were for her; the voices irritated because she was napping instead of responding to their demands.

Helen woke, a jolt crashing through her nervous system like an electric shock. For a moment, she wondered if there had been another earthquake, but the house was still—no vibration of walls and rattle of objects like a big truck passing by. In the months after the quake, she had tormented by such dreams—normal scenes interrupted by intense vibration, shaking her until she awoke in a state of cold terror.

She sat up, rubbed her eyes and scratched her belly. She remained sitting in bed for more several minutes, wondering what time it was and trying to figure out if it were morning or evening. She looked down and realized she was in jeans and a

T-shirt. She remembered that she had only been napping. She hadn't meant to sleep so deeply, and she certainly hadn't meant to dream, especially one so vivid and apropos.

The dream had started with her driving her car over the route 27, back from Alta Lara, though she couldn't remember why she had been there. There was no one in the passenger seat. Tim and her grandfather were in the back. They were on the windiest part of route 27, the downhill section right after the crest. Despite her efforts to control it, her car kept going faster and faster. The brakes didn't really seem to work. Tim and her grandfather didn't seem concerned, though—they just talked in low voices about how typical it was and how Helen was always getting into these kinds of scrapes. She couldn't hear much of what they said, just a low murmur of disapproval. At some point, Joseph Harkes joined them in the car, and he too seemed utterly unconcerned that Helen's Volvo was uncontrollably careening down route 27's serpent-like curves, somehow keeping from either going over the barrier or plowing into the line of semi-trailer trucks on the other side. He was talking about the car as a symbol for life, and how driving was symbolic of how someone deals with it. Tim and her grandfather couldn't stop agreeing at how true it really was, that Joseph had hit the nail on the head. Tim kept saying, "it's so perfect, it's just so perfect" over and over. Finally Helen got so angry she let go of the steering wheel and yelled at them to shut up. Helen thought she would crash, but the car seemed to have a mind of its own, and they shot even faster down the curves approaching Welsh Valley. It was obvious that very soon they were all going to be killed in a horrible accident and it was all her fault, but Helen found herself to be oddly accepting of it all, as if it were exactly what she had expected would happen.

Helen shook her head, trying to dispel it from her mind. Couldn't her brain cells cut her some slack? Life was hard enough without these psychologically revealing dreams. She got it; Tim and Joseph Harkes were similar. She didn't need her subconscious to tell her that.

Through the wall, she heard the sound of a cupboard door being open and shut. She realized that someone else had returned to house. Bleary eyed, Helen got out of bed and exited her bedroom. Once in the kitchen, she saw Gretchen crouched in a corner. "Hey, Gretch'," Helen said.

Gretchen was picking through potatoes one by one in the torn mesh bag. A few potatoes had spilled out on to the floor. One in the corner, Helen saw, had been there long enough to sprout a curly green shoot. Helen shook her head slowly. Now that she was more awake, her stomach ached from hunger, but she had just lost her appetite, watching Gretchen pick through the moldy potatoes. Why did she live like this? Her home was slowly decaying into a hovel. It had never been like this the year before.

"Hey, Hel," Gretchen mumbled.

Helen sat at the table and ran her hand through the pile of mail that Gretchen must have just brought in. On top was an angry looking letter from Western Bell–no doubt a disconnection notice. To her surprise, she saw a hand-addressed envelope beneath it. From one David Stone, in Winterton, Mass. She felt a deep pang of unexpected dread inside of her, and shoved the letter under the pile of Victoria's Secrets catalogs. She hoped Gretchen wouldn't ask her about it.

"How was school?" Helen asked.

"Shitty. Life sucks."

"Yeah it does."

Gretchen stood up and showed Helen two potatoes. "Dinner," she said.

"Oh, boy."

Gretchen went to the sink. She took a stack of plates off the counter and put them onto another stack in the sink. It teetered and hit the back of the sink with a loud clink.

"Where's Bristle?" Helen asked. She hadn't seen her cat since she had come home.

"I saw her outside, playing in the garden next door."

"I'm worried about her roaming around this street. There are so many weird people around."

"She needs food."

"I know. We need to go to the grocery store, but I have no money."

"I thought you were going to the job center."

"I will, this week. It's just that I have no time."

"Yeah."

After rinsing off a knife, Gretchen sliced the potatoes into round discs. "There are messages for you on the answering service," she said.

"From who?"

"I don't know. I think one of them is Alice."

"Oh, I can't talk to her right now. I haven't returned her last three phone calls."

"Can I erase them?"

"Sure, go ahead. I don't care. I have nothing to say to anyone."

Helen and Gretchen sat across from each other, eating boiled potatoes covered with what remained of their butter, along with some salt and pepper from packets Helen had taken from Claimstake Pancakes.

In the living room played Helen's tape of the *Repo Man* soundtrack, which Peter had made for her during their freshman year. It had been part of Peter's effort to convince

Helen that there was some music that he liked that she liked as well, since she had gotten so tired of him talking about R.E.M. It had succeeded. Helen didn't really dislike R.E.M. that much, but there was something about Peter's almost religious devotion to them that irritated Helen. She loved to mock them, especially their incomprehensibly whiny and sentimental lyrics, all delivered in a sing-song mumble that was supposed to be profound but just made Helen feel sleepy, and wanting to listen to AC/DC or The Cult, or something else that just rocked with no bones about it.

"So what's up?" Helen asked. "I haven't seen you all week."

Helen had only eaten half a potato, and she was already bored with it. She forced her jaw to continue chewing. She tore open the last salt packet and sprinkled it on them. If you put enough salt, you could make anything edible.

"Not much. I was at Bill's house."

"And how's he doing?" Helen asked, hoping the answer was that he had terminal cancer and that was why Gretchen had been spending so much time with him, comforting him in his last hours as he slipped from this world to the next.

"He's good," Gretchen replied neutrally.

"Now that Todd and I are history, you should break up with Bill. Be single with me," Helen said. "It's not so bad."

"That would sort of make sense," Gretchen said. "If you had broken up with Todd. And not the other way around."

"Well..." Helen said. "Shit. What does that have to do with it?"

"Just making a point," Gretchen said matter-of-factly.

"If he hadn't broken up with me, I would have. I just couldn't think of a way to tell him."

Gretchen gave her a skeptical look, her cheeks bulging as she chewed, which made her look like an evil squirrel. She swallowed, and said, "As I recall, you weren't even speaking to him."

"I was getting over that," Helen replied. "I was gonna call him. In any case, you should still break up with Bill," Helen said briskly, deciding that logic was not going to help her. She hated arguing–it always felt like such a waste of time. The truth was the truth. And was it worth hurting someone's feelings just to prove a point?

"Maybe I will," Gretchen said. "Maybe I won't. What have you got against Bill, anyway? You never say much to him when he's over here."

Helen didn't where to even begin listing everything she disliked about Bill, so she didn't bother. "I just don't think he's the right guy for you."

"You just don't hang out with us enough to see his good side," Gretchen said.

Helen thought that the only way Gretchen could make her see Bill's good side, was if she went with her to the morgue to identify his body. "He's a drunkard!" Helen exclaimed. "And he's mean to you," she added in a more serious voice.

"So he gets drunk a lot," Gretchen said. "So do your friends."

Jake, Peter, and Mick had made a bad impression on Gretchen at the beginning of fall quarter–somehow she had ended up having to clean up the front steps after a night of partying, a toxic stew of cigarette butts, bong water, tobacco, spilled beer and finally, courtesy of Peter, a nice coating of vomit. Helen had really meant to clean up the mess, but she had ended up staying at Todd's that night, needing to sleep and unable to deal with the party in her own house. It hadn't been an ideal beginning to Gretchen's tenancy at Holly Street.

"Yeah..." Helen said. "I guess we all are. Speaking of which, I want a beer."

"You can come with me to Bill's house. He's got some."

"Shine," Helen said. She got up and put her now empty plate in the sink. Gretchen just wasn't able to deal with the fact that her boyfriend was an asshole. Well, at least she had made an effort. Without staying more, Helen exited the kitchen, trying to think of some other way to procrastinate so she didn't have to face *Las Mujeres de la Nubes.*

Back in her room, Helen looked at the framed picture on her dresser. Taken by Roxy, it showed Jessica and Lana on either side of Helen, with their arms around each other, standing in front of their new house on Holly Street. It had been taken the day when Roxy and Jessica had just arrived from LA, having driven up in Roxy's white VW Rabbit. Lana had come the day before, having been driven down from Galena in Sophie's yellow Volvo station wagon. Lana's hair was still long, and they all looked pretty much as they had freshman year, though Helen liked her hair a lot more (she has splurged right before the left Alta Lara and gotten her hair cut at the same place Sarah did).

That picture had marked the end of what had been a magical time. She had already been in the house for two weeks (their rental had started September 1st, and now that she was paying rent, Helen was determined to get every penny's worth). The day she moved in, she had gotten back in touch with Todd, who had just gotten a house with his friends John Wray and Brent Skranslatt on St. Petersburg St., near the west-side Safeway.

Todd was a guy she had only known casually up to that point. The first time she had met him had been on one of their Friday night expeditions to Dorm II. Dorm I and II both partied incessantly, since they the two Kane College dorms filled mostly with freshmen—or fresh-people, as you were supposed to call them at UCSZ–but there seemed to be a subtle difference in the characters of the two dormitories. Maybe there were more stoners and Deadheads in Dorm I, while surfers dominated in Dorm II. Maybe it was because the beer of choice in Dorm I was Old Milwaukee, while in Dorm II it was Schmidt Sport Packs. It was hard to say.

In any case, they periodically made trips over to Dorm II to scope out the filet, as Roxy put it. They would psyche themselves up by listening to "Doug's La Di Da Di" while doing up their hair, fending off Jake, George and Sophie's attempts to make them take bong hits all the while. The night Helen had met Todd it had been just Helen, Roxy, and Lana, squired by Tim. It turned out to be an epic one, because Roxy had scammed with Neil, Helen had met Todd, and Lana had slept with some guy whose name now escaped Helen, but who lived on the third floor, the same section as Missy.

Helen was the one who had invited Tim along. Roxy had been opposed–she didn't mind Tim, but he was kind of geeky and not really compatible with the Dorm II crowd, but Helen had wanted him along. Roxy was on the hunt, but Helen didn't really feel like she was entitled to be, given the ambiguous state of her relationship with Dave Stone.

When they arrived at the third floor, the halls were crowded with people. In the last room on the left, they found Neil and Todd. They were bent over the dresser, backs to the door. Tim, virginal in all respects, and Lana, country girl that she was, were both cheerfully oblivious, but Helen and Roxy could tell that they had been doing lines. They ended up talking to Todd and Neil while Tim tried to impress Lana with his knowledge of global politics. It didn't take long for Todd and Neil to start paying Helen and Roxy some serious attention.

The night had gone on from there, and Helen was sure that if she had had just one more beer she would have ended up with Todd, but at the critical moment, she rejoined Tim (engrossed in a discussion about which Smiths album was the best) and kept him by her side. Not too much later, they returned to Dorm I, leaving Roxy to consummate her tryst with Neil on the picnic table in the corner of the roof. Lana had long since disappeared, only to do the walk of shame the next morning between the two dorms, and then interrupting Sophie and George in the middle of the act. All in all, a very scandalous night, and morning after.

After that, Helen and Todd were casual acquaintances, and everyone in Dorm II, at least, expected them to soon become more than that. She found herself hanging out on Friday and Saturday nights in Dorm II. When she was there, Helen felt like a star, like the queen of the world. In Dorm I, she was with her friends from high school, and had to do whatever Jake wanted, because everyone followed his lead. Everyone looked to Jake to set the social agenda, and didn't seem capable of thinking on their own. In Dorm II, though, she was the center of it all. She would walk into a room, arms all around her, half-hugs, squeezes, laughs, introductions to everyone by Todd, who never lost interest in introducing her around. She knew she shouldn't like it so much, but she did. David had always been so calm, so self-contained. They would hang out at a party, and he would do the right things, but Helen never got the feeling he was proud to be with her, that it made a difference. He probably would have had just as good a time, maybe better, if she stayed home–as long as Jake, Peter and Todd Forrest were there, that was all that mattered. Todd, though, fed off her beauty and the attentive glances of other guys. They coveted her, and she liked it. Todd enjoyed it, too, and that made her like it even more.

Helen knew on some level that Todd and his cronies weren't as nice as her old friends, that it was all completely superficial, and she couldn't talk to them like she could talk to

Tim, or Roxy, or Jessica. But that was also a relief, in a way. She didn't have to worry about hurt feelings or saying the wrong thing. Conversations stayed light, and kept short, constantly interrupted by some new arrival, gossip, impromptu drinking challenge.

Looking back, it amazed her that she and Todd didn't get together that spring. A lot of it had to do with Jake and her old friends—she was afraid they would think she was a slut and a bitch, and of what they would say to David. As the following summer had gone by, Helen found herself more and more irritated that she had let her faithfulness to David stop her from pursuing Todd, once their relationship had ended soon after both were back for the summer in Alta Lara.

At least she had been smart enough to keep her options open. Helen and Todd had exchanged phone numbers at the end of spring quarter, and spoken twice with vague aspirations of meeting up in the city, but their schedules had never worked out. Helen had been only too willing to drive up to the city and hang out with him, but he seemed busy, and a small, nasty voice in the back of her mind told her he already had a girl to occupy his attentions, and didn't need to motivate for her.

Once Helen returned to Santa Zita for her sophomore year, she decided to give him a call. She convinced him to come over and help her move her dresser, which after two days she had decided really needed to be on the other side of the room. She cooked him dinner, they drank red wine on the sofa, and nature took care of the rest. She remembered the wonderful luxury of having her own room, to be able to take their time and spend the night together with no worrying about being interrupted, disturbing Jessica, or anything else. It had been a good way to christen her new house.

Looking back, that time seemed like the high point of her life so far. It had been so nice to be away from Alta Lara, away from friends who had more money than she did and didn't have to worry about financial aid, getting a job, or finding a place to live that wouldn't bankrupt them utterly, which gave them more time to be disapproving of Helen and how she lived her life–who she slept with, and why. Away from David Stone and his silent disapproval, the awkwardness of dealing with him and the feeling that there was a standard he carried around in his head that he had applied to Helen, which she had failed to live up to. Jake, Peter and Sarah bumming on her because David was bummed.

Worse, both Peter and Tim knew that she had broken up with David, and she knew desire for her still flickered in both of them. She had been particularly offended by Peter's attentions. He managed to have both his cake and eat it too, by bumming on her for hurting his friend, but also being psyched that maybe now he had his chance with her, like she was some bottle to be passed around the circle until everyone drank their fill. His hypocrisy drove her crazy, and she found almost any excuse not to speak to him.

Tim was subtler, but in a way that was more disappointing, since she had thought by the end of freshman year that he had gotten over her. She had tried hard to set him up with Alice, or even Sarah, both eager for new boyfriends so they could avoid rehashing their high school experiences, but they just hadn't seemed to engage his interest, at least romantically. He didn't seem interested in dating, or even boning down with them all night long, which is what they all really needed, in Helen's humble opinion. Tim and Sarah had, under the influence, gone so far as to kiss, but after that, Tim had faded into the background and though Sarah had told Helen she liked Tim, she had not made the kind of effort that Helen had seen her make with other guys, like Todd Forrest.

Once Helen and David had broken up, Tim had hinted, in his oh-so-clever and enigmatic way, that he still carried a torch for her. He had come and met her for lunch in downtown Alta Lara, when she was working at Those Shoes. For some unearthly reason, he had brought a bouquet of flowers. They went to the Good Earth for sandwiches loaded with enough alfalfa to feed a herd of goats, then got gelato. The atmosphere had been oddly tense, like Tim had something to say but he couldn't make himself get to the point. Helen had gotten a dreadful feeling he was going to make some kind of huge declaration of love, and she started talking about the most asinine things in order to forestall the excruciating awkwardness of that conversation. She found herself extolling the virtues of Tom Cruise's acting in *Cocktail,* something she would never have done under ordinary circumstances.

Tim then walked back to his father's house, leaving her to endure the interrogation of her co-worker, Jody, another Alta Lara High class of '87 graduate, about why she'd received a bouquet, and that Tim wasn't a beau, or even a potential one, but just a friend. It was sweet, but also kind of inexplicable and weirdly embarrassing. Didn't he realize that she had no place to put flowers at work? She worked retail, it wasn't like she had a desk or cubicle to put them on. She didn't say that, though. Instead, she pointed out that Alice had called her the day before, wondering what was going on that weekend and that she had no plans. That hint, though, was lost on Tim, since he immediately interpreted her to mean that they should all hang together, plus they should call Jake, because, God knows, you couldn't possibly have any fun without Jake somehow being involved.

By the end of the summer, every one of her friends in Alta Lara was driving her crazy for different reasons. Their tight-knit group was starting to suffocate her. Compared to that, end of the summer in Santa Zita was a whole new world of possibilities–her own house, car, no job, Jessica and Roxy on the way for the non-judgmental female company she was craving–but most of all, Todd.

Now she was alone. She had neither David nor Todd. She wished it could be then, and not now. She felt the longing to go back in time as she closed her eyes, like a child praying to God to make the rainy day go away. Was her whole life just going to be downhill from the fall of 1988? That just couldn't be so. She wasn't even 21 yet. All of this self-pity was ridiculous.

She remembered David's letter. She should read it. She went back into the kitchen and retrieved from under the pile of junk mail. With a mixture of hope and dread, she slit the top of the envelope with a bread knife and withdrew the pages of notebook paper within.

Helen tossed the letter from David aside, turned the reading lamp by her bed off, rolled over on her back, and stared at the ceiling. She felt even lonelier now, monstrously alone. David's irritatingly complacent letter had been full of news–about his friends at BU, his studies, playing Ultimate Frisbee and his plans for studying abroad in Spain during spring quarter. When Helen had first seen the return address, she had felt a pang of dread–for some reason, she felt the only reason David would be writing her a letter was to say that he had met the love of his life; that everything he had felt for Helen had just been a rehearsal for this, the real thing.

Once she read the letter, though, and that turned out to not be the case, she wondered if she might have felt better if he had mentioned that he had a girlfriend. Somehow the utter lack of mention of his love life drove her crazy. She could just imagine him thinking as he wrote: "see, Helen, we broke up and now I don't even need someone. I don't have to be in a relationship to be happy. I can be happy without love. Unlike you." He was strong, self-reliant; he needed only himself.

But she had seen him be weak. He had eagerly crawled into bed with her last Fourth of July, despite the fact she was with Todd Fox. She smiled to herself. That had been quite a night. They had missed the fireworks at Moffet Field (the reason she had told Alice why she was going to Alta Lara with him), but made more than enough themselves. David was fit, with great endurance, less prone to experiencing difficulties due to over-consumption. He had demonstrated his abilities that night in his empty house, his parents gone to celebrate July Fourth at Lake Tahoe. They had done it in his parent's bed, since David still had the same single bed he had had since the eighth grade in his room, which, along with Helen's infidelity to Todd, gave the night an extra spice. It had been a wonderful exercise in nostalgia, worth the skeptical glances she'd had to endure from Jessica and Tim in the following weeks. A high point of that crazy summer of '89, which Tim apparently thought was so cool, and couldn't let go of. It was already starting to seem like a long time ago.

What was David doing right now? She hoped he was alone, that he was secretly jacking off and wishing he was with her. Helen had always been vaguely turned on by that notion, but had once made the mistake when they lived together of confessing it to Jessica and Tim. Tim had been both thrilled and embarrassed, like he was so much of the time, but her best friend had been appalled; first that a man would do something like that, and second that Helen had thought of it, and sort of liked it. Sometimes Jessica surprised her–despite her sensitivity and intelligence, she sometimes didn't seem to completely get men–they were somehow alien to her. Maybe because she had grown up with only sisters; the middle of three, like Jan on the Brady Bunch. Helen had no brothers, either, but then, she was an only child, so she was just a freak, in a lot of ways. She had certainly always been surrounded by boys from the earliest age. She had been a tomboy as a child, preferring playing in the mud to arranging furniture in dollhouses, and once she passed into puberty, she had acquired other qualities that guaranteed her masculine attention.

That didn't change the fact that she was alone, too. Helen wondered if she should try masturbating–it had been a while, and she was out of practice. It seemed like so much work, though. A guy could just buy a dirty magazine and get some quick relief, but she had to imagine something nice, something real and romantic, and that just triggered the same feeling of loneliness she was trying to get away from. No escape there.

Instead, she would just lie here and stare at the water stains in the corner of her room's ceiling until something happened. Maybe they would have another earthquake, this time big enough that it laid waste to the entire city and campus. School would be canceled forever, and matters would be taken out of her hands. No one could blame her for moving to Montana then. The water stains were grey blotches, lit by the faint orange glow of the streetlights outside, reflected off the low blanket of fog that covered Santa Zita that night.

Six

That fog remained the next morning as she walked along Holly Street towards Redwood` and the bus stop. She passed by the vacant lot where the house had burned down the night of the Yaçoan quake, the event that had forced the evacuation of their street. The firefighters had told Helen and Gretchen the whole block might go up in flames, telling them to hurry as they desperately tried to find a hydrant that still produced water.

The outline of that house remained in the form of a line of bricks in the ground, partially hidden by weeds and grasses. She had never liked the people in the house that had been there. She, Jessica, and Lana had spent many hours trying to decide if it was a crack house, brothel, or both, but it still made her feel sorry.

The neglected ruins just reminded her of how much downtown Santa Zita had changed–no more Bookshop Santa Zita, Miller House, Santa Zita Coffee Roasting Company, Eztel's Department Store, all collapsed and torn down; just empty holes in the ground. Even buildings that had looked fine from the outside had been leveled, since they were apparently unsafe, too internally damaged to be worth saving. So much lost in one minute, a whole world taken away. She had seen pictures in the *Santa Zita Guardian* of the new buildings planned for downtown, and they looked like they belonged in Silicon Valley office parks. The city would never be the same again.

Thinking of the earthquake and its aftermath made her think of Tim. Somehow the quake seemed to mark the time when Tim had started to fade from her life. He had never called her about Wednesday night. She had thought about calling him, but something stopped her. If he didn't want to hang out, he didn't want to hang out. That was all there was to it. She had made the effort, and it had not been reciprocated. Helen gritted her teeth and resolved to think no more about the day and her solitary condition. She didn't need Todd, and she didn't need Tim, and she wasn't going to need any man ever again if she could help it.

Helen's resolve to not think about Valentine's Day lasted until her bus-ride to campus was half-over, when she saw a guy get on the bus, carrying a bouquet of blood red roses. Helen wondered who was the lucky girl–receiving such a traditional Valentine's Day gesture at that most anti-romantic of places, UCSZ.

The bus roared uphill, past the east remote parking lot and the athletic fields. Helen looked and saw the fog receding overhead; the promise of a sunny day visible in the shimmering blue waters of the Terra Nueva Bay. Clouds still crowded the mountains above Terra Nueva, giving it the appearance of a mythical isle, one with only a tenuous connection to the rest of the world. The cloud-wreathed peaks beckoned to Helen; a place of rest after death. She would be borne there by faeries, her body covered with flowers, leaving only her face and hair free, shining forever, perfectly preserved. They would come and pay homage to her, their fallen queen.

Today would be the first time she had gone to a Latin American Women Writers lecture in a month. At this stage of her life, a morning class just wasn't fitting in. Not only had she not been going, but she hadn't read any of the books that had been assigned. Not one. There was a mid-term coming in less than two weeks, and Helen was dreading it. It wasn't a take-home, but in-class, which meant she and Gretchen (who had actually been doing the reading) couldn't collaborate. She needed to hit the books, big time.

The bus halted at the Fremont College stop with huffs and squeaks from the hydraulics. Helen, along with just about everybody else on the bus, crowded out on to the sidewalk. Helen saw the guy carrying the roses march purposefully ahead of the crowd in the direction of Fremont College's dorms. She wondered if he would get what he wanted. Would his twenty dollars get him to the promised land? Or was he already there, and the roses were just a tax he paid to keep it that way? She was being cynical. She hated Valentine's Day.

♋

After Latin American Women Writers, Helen got coffee at the Fremont College coffee shop and walked to the library. To save money, she was planning on reading some of the class's texts there instead of buying them. Her professor claimed there were plenty of copies available.

As she approached the library, two freshman girls came at her from the opposite direction, talking much too excitedly for that time of morning. One girl was blond, the other brunette–and the blond girl looked faintly familiar, though Helen couldn't place her. She was tall and pretty, but in an attainable way. Helen was sure that whatever dorm she lived in, she was breaking plenty of hearts.

"What drink are you making?" the blond girl asked.

"Sex on the beach, of course. You can't have a chain party without sex on the beach. Who's buying, anyway?"

"Amy's going with that guy on her floor. He's a junior."

Good for them, she thought. No romantic dinner or relationship worries for them. Just mass drunkenness and commitment-less scamming. Her freshman year had only been two years ago–why did it feel like so much longer? She wished the only thing she had to worry about was finding someone old enough to buy alcohol.

Once at the library, Helen asked for the book at the short-term lending desk. Amazingly, there was one copy left. Helen took the tattered volume of short stories and went to one of the long tables perpendicular to the floor to ceiling tinted windows that looked out into the primordial tangle of the ferns, shrubs and redwood tree. She opened the book, stared at the first page of the first story, and yawned so abruptly and forcefully she sprayed the book with saliva. Mortified, Helen wiped the page as dry as she could, then resolved to rest her eyes for a few minutes.

Helen awoke as she had so many times in the past six months, to the sound and sensation of vibration. This was one of the times when it was real. She raised her head, hearing the clatter of the metal bookshelves and the roar of thousands of tons of concrete vibrating all around her. After a still pause filled with loud exclamations, the building shook again. That was the worst thing about the aftershocks–they came in swarms. The second passed quickly, leaving Helen's heart fluttering and her brain completely unable to concentrate, feelings and memories oscillating like the palpitations in her chest.

She hated the aftershocks. Not only did they make her recall the raw visceral terror of the Yaçoan quake, but they also made her think of Todd. She and Todd had had one of their worst fights the night of the earthquake. After they had been evacuated from Holly Street, they had been told it wouldn't be safe for them to return until the next day, at the earliest.

Helen had gone to Todd's house, which was on the west side where hardly anything had been damaged at all. She had wanted him to let Gretchen and Ellery stay there as well, instead of camping out on the Santa Zita High football field, which was what the cops were telling the Holly Street residents to do. He refused, and a little later Helen realized why–he wanted to have endless sex by candlelight. He told her he thought the blackout was sexy. She had accused him of being insensitive, reminded him that people had died that day. One of the girls who had died when the brick wall of the Bookshop Santa Zita had fallen on the Santa Zita Coffee Roasting Company had been a friend of of Ellery's. It so easily could have been her, or Jessica, or any one of their friends. How many times had she gone there to get coffee when she worked at Sunshine? Todd had tried to make some pseudo-intellectual argument about sex and death that had just turned her stomach.

Helen had given in, finally. Hating herself as Todd pushed himself into her. When sex with Todd was bad, it could be really bad. This was one of those times. Helen had the distinct impression that by the time they had finished fighting, Todd's ardor had faded and he only went through with it to prove a point. Sometimes make-up sex could be really good, but not this time. It didn't help that it seemed like every five minutes there was an aftershock that rattled the house. Helen couldn't really sleep that night. Every time Helen was on the verge of sleep, a quick waking dream of vibration would snap her awake, heart pounding, sweat dripping out of her armpits, reliving the terror of the quake as if it were the first time.

Exactly how she felt now, staring at the ceiling tile, wondering if it were possible that the aftershock could cause cracks hidden in the library to bring it all crashing down. Campus officials had claimed all of the buildings on campus could withstand a quake of any magnitude, since they had been built after stricter building codes had been passed, but what if the contractors had been dishonest? Helen didn't trust what the campus administration had to say.

Helen passed through the shaded space between two of Fremont College's four-story dorms and emerged into blinding rays of light, from the setting sun piercing through a gap in the fog over the Terra Nueva Bay. She squinted and tried to clear the spots from her vision. When she could open her eyes all the way, she saw a familiar lock of black hair above dark brown eyes, like a comma tipped over on its side, moving towards her, recognizing her at exactly the same moment.

Without thinking, and realizing she didn't want to as she did, Helen stopped.

"Hey, Helen," Todd said.

"Hi, Todd, how are you?"

"Doing okay. Going home?"

"Yeah."

"Cool, cool. How's being a TA?"

"Great. I've got a really cool section. I like my students. It's working out well." Helen smiled to indicate just how well it was going, hoping to let Todd know that even though it was challenging, she was holding up.

"I'm happy for you. Oh, by the way, my house is having a party this Friday night. You're invited, of course. Bring your friends. Tell Jessica."

"Uh, sure. Thanks."

"So, any plans for tonight?" he said, his brown eyes glinting, so dark they were almost black.

Asking it like it was just any night–when he knew perfectly well it was Valentine's Day. Helen breathed through her nose, trying to calm herself. "Yeah, I do."

"Same with me. I'm just going to be hanging out–with Karen, you remember her."

The words were spoken carelessly, but Helen caught the cold gleam in Todd's eyes. It was all so lame, and so fucking predictable. Karen was a friend of Willoughby the surfer dude. Todd used to flirt with her at parties whenever he felt like Helen was paying too much attention to Tim, or Jake, or whatever guy she happened to be talking to at the time. She and Missy had been room-mates freshman year–in fact it was in their room that Helen had first met Todd. While Karen wasn't quite as much of a slut as Missy, she had been around the block more than a few times. If Todd wanted her, she would do him. But even so, Helen felt her heart beat faster and a pit well up in her belly. Todd had someone to be with on Valentine's Day, and she didn't. No matter how much of a better person she was than Todd or Karen, nothing could change that simple fact.

"I'm sure you'll have a good time. I... don't have any plans," Helen heard herself saying. She had wanted to lie, but her brain was paralyzed, forcing her to imagine Todd and Karen together. Her humiliation was complete.

"Great," Todd said absently, as if she had just told him some amazing plan.

"Look," Todd, "I've got to go–"

"Sure, I need to jam, too. Nice to run into you."

Helen hurried away, before her body could betray her further. Since he had left the message dumping her, she had imagined a thousand times the next time they saw each other. Instead of clawing his eyes out, which was what she had envisioned doing the first week after their break-up, it had seemed so civilized. At least, for him–she was sure he would've already forgotten about it fifteen minutes later. While her day, week, and possibly life, were ruined by this two-minute encounter. Already she was forced by her imagination to imagine Todd with Karen–his pleasure in her company, the sound of his breathe in her ear, her head on his chest, their post-coital contentment.

Todd's ability to turn on her attraction for him at will, even with the most transparently lame maneuvers, made the blood pound in her brain. Whenever he wanted, he could become the person she had originally been so attracted to. She had to stay away from him. That was the only solution.

Fifteen minutes later, Helen waited, along with many others, for the county bus, endlessly replaying the scene with Todd in her head. For a few minutes she had tried to convince herself it didn't matter, that Valentine's Day was just something concocted by greeting card companies, that Todd was an asshole, and that relationships were all bullshit anyway, but the endlessly repeating vision in her mind, seemingly in time with the pounding of her heart, had driven out those thoughts. It was starting to make her physically ill. Worse, she was feeling the pinpricks in the corner of her eyes, and a lump in her throat. Everything was just so fucked. Tim wouldn't hang out with her, Todd had Karen to fuck, and she was just alone, with nothing to do and no one to do it with.

The bus stopped, the blue and yellow beach and sunset logo of the Santa Zita County transit system right in front of her. Helen found herself carried along with the crowd of students heading home for the day, a wave of humanity that she was too tired to resist. She felt a murderous anger towards their normality and happy chatter when she just wanted to be alone and away from everything.

She got one of the last completely empty seats left on the bus, three quarters of the way to the back. Helen hoped she wouldn't have to share the seat, because she was sure anyone who looked at her close up would realize she was only holding tears back through strength of will.

The bus stopped at Church and Redwood. A young Hispanic woman got on, carrying a baby. The baby was crying spasmodically. The bus quieted, as everyone tried to ignore the baby's unbelievable unhappiness. With dread, Helen realized the only empty seat on the bus was next to her. Sure enough, the woman sat next to her.

Out of the corner of her eye, Helen saw the woman give her a small, hopeful smile, as if to ask forgiveness. Helen just stared straight ahead, unable to deal. Of all things, a baby. A baby crying hysterically. She just couldn't handle it. She looked at the little thing, in its swaddling clothes, as the woman tried to comfort it by murmuring sing-song words in Spanish. To no avail, as the infant just cried and cried its guts out, almost choking on its own tears. Helen spent a minute studying it, feeling revulsion she didn't think she was capable of. The woman looked at her with a worried, embarrassed expression. Despite the fact that they were around the same age, Helen felt the gulf between them, and realized she might envy Helen because she went to college and didn't have the burden of a child.

Helen stared out the window, trying to concentrate on that and only that. She felt another wave of sadness sweep over her, sadness for herself and for the world, where love was doomed and all children were unhappy. Like vomiting and yawning, crying was contagious. Despite her attempts to block them out, the baby's hysterical sobs were breaking through and eroding Helen's walls within. She had thought she might be able to hold back the tears until she got home, but she thought now they might pour out in front of the bus, the woman, in front of all of them. The final humiliation: incontinent with tears. This is what Todd had made her into, how he made her feel about herself. She clenched her fists, repeated "I will not cry" in a silent whisper over and over, in rhythm with the baby's screams. The rest of the bus was silent.

She felt trapped, in the back of the bus, surrounded by people she didn't know and didn't want to know. All she wanted was for the ride to be over, but it went on and on. The bus crept down Church St. stopping every block for seemingly no reason. It was all Helen could do to not scream out in frustration at the driver. What the fuck is wrong with you? Can't you even drive a bus right? Did every little thing have to go against her? Every person, every action, every moment?

The only thing that stopped her was that if she opened her mouth, she thought the delicate balance in her body would be altered and the tears would come, uncontrolled. She almost grabbed her jaw and held it in place with her hand, trying to stop the bawling that was building within. It was so strong she though it might tear a hole in her belly and burst out, leaving her nothing but an empty husk, a used up incubator for the murderous spirit that had been unleashed on the world.

What kind of a world was it where Todd could cause her so much pain and not know it, not care, not have to feel responsible? He was a monster. And yet he was happy, so much happier than Helen, than the woman beside her, then most of the women she knew. He didn't deserve it, he deserved to rot in the lowest level of Hell, have his guts picked apart by vultures, his penis sliced off by a she-demon's talon and his testicles consumed by writhing worms. But there was no justice in the world. People did what they did, and if they had power they used it, and if you didn't you just suffered until the day you couldn't take it any more and you hurled yourself in front of a speeding passenger train.

A new and even louder eruption of sobs made Helen's eyes glance involuntarily at the baby next to her. How could something so defenseless, and ugly, that spent all of its time mewling, burping, and shitting, ever grow up to be anything more? She didn't like babies. They scared her. They required constant attention. It was worse than having a pet. They needed you, and without your constant care, they would just die. She was never ever going to have a child, ever. She swore to herself, made an oath in her mind, to God if He existed and was watching and listening to the thoughts in her mind. She couldn't imagine bringing a child into a world like this, with men like Todd running it.

Helen wondered if that was how her mother felt about her, something that happened and gotten in her way; made her stay with her father longer than she would have otherwise. Her mother couldn't just move out, she needed support, money. The product of a loveless marriage, she never should have been brought into the world.

The bus slowed again and stopped. Another shuffling line of people got on. No matter who they were—old people, teenagers, housewives—all seemed to take forever to pay. It was the same every time, stop, doors open, people entered, then a few moments of motion, followed by exactly the same thing again. Helen couldn't take it anymore.

"Excuse me," she said in a gasping voice.

The young woman pressed her howling baby to her chest and quickly moved out of Helen's way, looking at Helen fearfully as if she thought Helen might injure her infant. Helen said nothing to her, but charged up the aisle, grabbing the seat handles as the bus swayed.

"I missed my stop, can I please get off here?" Helen said loudly. Her voice came out in an imperious screech, which caused those near the driver to look down and away in embarrassment, but Helen had stopped caring what people thought of her. The bus driver, glaring at her with a mixture of confusion and irritation, slowed the bus and opened the door. "Fine, get off."

Helen scrambled off, in the middle of the steep downhill incline of Redwood Street, just a few blocks from Holly. The moment she stepped off the bus, the dam broke and she felt the hot tears stream down her face. She wiped her face repeatedly with the back of her hand, but they just kept coming. She could barely see well enough to avoid the places where tree branches had broken through the surface of the sidewalk, and the cracks from the quake that still hadn't been fixed.

A cold wind blew in from the ocean, making her eyes sting and water even more. She had to stop and soak her eyes with her sleeve before she could continue. She saw her house, dusty ochre yellow. The lights were off, to her relief. That was all she wanted right now–a dark house, and a bed to cry on.

The tears had finally run out. Helen lay on her bed, staring at the ceiling, breathing shallowly in and out. The last light had faded from the south-western sky. The hot anger and grief seemed to have run out of her, through her tear ducts and on to the pillow. She felt worn out and hollow now. The anger that had devoured her insides had consumed everything with her and fled, searching for somewhere else to nest.

Helen got off her bed and went to the bathroom. She washed her face thoroughly. When she was done, she examined herself in the mirror. She took off the shirt, still damp with sweat and tears. She ran a finger down her shoulders, and traced the outline of her white bra.

How could someone she loved, and who had professed to love her, turn out to be such an asshole? The world couldn't be like that, it just couldn't. But maybe it was.

She saw clearly now. The world was just a machine, and nobody really cared about anybody else. So why should she? Why are you being so silly? she asked herself. If being with Karen is all Todd needs, then that's all you need, too. You're attractive. Men want you. You know they do. Why should she let Todd win?

Helen swore to herself that she was going to live her life without Todd. If he was going to get laid, then so was she. If he had a heart of stone, then she would harden herself as well. She would start living her life even if it killed her.

When I shared this draft of Helen of Santa Zita with the writing group I was part of from 2002 to 2005, they reacted quite negatively to the character of Helen. I was surprised, even a bit shocked, by that at the time. Now, though, I can see that this piece is probably the most bathetic (which may or may not be a real word) my writing ever got.

I wanted Helen of Santa Zita to feel like you were right with Helen, in the moment with her thoughts, but she might not be the right kind of character for that. It's a difficult challenge to depict a character feeling sad, self-pitying, and at wit's end without making them unlikable; a challenge I'm not sure I rose to.

Of course, there are techniques one can use to get around that problem—a common one is to have the character telling their story from later in their life, when they have some distance and perspective. Otherwise the reader becomes an unwitting therapist, forced to listen to never-ending tales of woe, without at least getting paid for their time.

That's probably the reason, other than the fact that I told myself I needed to stop getting distracted from 1989/Celebrated Summer, *that I didn't finish this book. That's not to say I might not revisit this material someday in the future, but it would likely be in a very different form, or combined with the Tim-centric sequel to* The Deep and Savage Way *I have also contemplated.*

Not long after I finished that draft of Helen of Santa Zita, in late spring 2001, I left for a trip to Australia to visit a friend who had been living there for six months, working their wine harvest. After spending some time in Sydney and a weekend in the Blue Mountains, we flew to Cairns, than took a bus further up the coast, to Port Douglas. We fell in love with that town, a perfect balance of civilized amenities and tropical isolation. About a week later, we took a mini-bus further up the coast to Cape Tribulation, so named because that was where Captain James Cook had come to grief in 1770.

While I was there I wrote a few notes, on the only day when my friend and I did separate activities–she had a lifelong dream to ride a horse on the beach, while I am completely terrified of them—which I later expanded up on my return. This story was based on what it was like to be in Port Douglas, feeling a million miles from anywhere, right when Dotcom was crashing, hard, and it felt like my life was, too, though I may not have wanted to admit it.

Port Douglas

She looked in the mirror and saw crow's feet by her eyes. She saw him behind her reflection, listening with earphones on, a look of rapturous wonder and concentration on his face. It was a look she hadn't seen on his face the whole trip–a look she hadn't seen since college. Nobody ever looked at anything like that in Chicago. It was ecstasy. She wanted to feel something like that.

"Remember this song?" he asked. He offered her the earphones. She recognized it. "Twelve years ago," he added.

Twelve years since that time. She turned back to the mirror. She patted her belly and focused her eyes on her reflection again. Rounder. Definitely a lot rounder. She was starting to fade in places. Someone like her mother looked back from the mirror.

She still had nice hair, though. It was one area where she had improved her looks since college. Back then, her hair had been an embarrassing rat's nest of mousy brown curls. Her hair was still curly, but now they were shinier, colored just the right shade of auburn, as bright as possible without looking fake. She had had them redone at her favorite place in Chicago the day before she left. It had been hard to get the appointment, but it had been worth it.

You could either be unattractive and have time to get dates, or work out and be so exhausted you could barely stay awake while you watched the movie you rented, alone. If you could spend the money to solve that dilemma, it was worth it.

They left their motel room and walked down Davidson Street, heading to the beach. They walked by a backpacker's café, several rows of beige monitors filling the windows. It looked like the floor of a brokerage house.

"Look at all the Internet computers," she said.

"No one escaped from dotcom," he said flatly.

"Are people really that addicted?"

"People like to feel connected."

"I guess. But always? And what are they connecting to?"

"Each other. Something more. The world beyond. Outside of them."

"They are in the world, though. They're here."

"Which is part of the world. But not all of it."

"Maybe it's all they should need," she said

"Maybe it should be. But it isn't."

Then she remembered she needed to email her cat-sitter. So they went in.

While she tapped on the ancient keyboard, old enough to still have that comforting metallic clicky-clack sound he remembered from his childhood, he visualized how the Internet café was set up. The computers were hooked via silver cables to an Ethernet router, which in turn connected to a firewall, and a DSL connection, most likely.

The packets containing the email she had just sent marched, guided by their own logic, from node to node to node, knowing where they needed to be. They could take different paths, but still arrive in the same place. From the DSL to the local phone company, down the coast, to wherever (Cairns? Brisbane? Sydney?) the transpacific cables originated, going straight across thousands of miles of muck, to Honolulu, and then crossing another unfathomable distance of seafloor to arrive at the San Francisco Bay Area, where it had all began. There they connected to the awesomely dense reticulum of trunks, local pipes and fiber optic that crisscrossed North America; not owned, controlled or even comprehended by any one person or entity. Even so, the packets she had sent, containing her email, would end up wherever they needed to be. Who was she emailing? Who did she need to feel connected to?

He smiled to himself. He felt no desire to check email. Just knowing the possibility of connection existed was enough, for now.

"Why are you smiling?" she asked.

He shrugged. "It's nice here," he said. "It makes you want to smile."

She had gotten back in touch with him by email. For that much, she had to admit, the Internet was useful. If she had called him, out of the blue after five years of no contact, it might have seemed weird. She had imagined that conversation and her visions of it could never get past the initial awkwardness. Email made it seem natural. Natural to him, at least, which was the important thing. He was too smart about people's motives for her to ever be anything less than cautious.

A mutual friend had given her his email address. She knew what he had been up to; that he had started a company and had some brief success, before it had all gone wrong.

She guessed that he might have some free time, now. She had been right. His reply to her email had come incredibly quickly–almost too fast, considering its length. He had always liked to write, she remembered. At her company, emails tended to be terse, ungrammatical and perfunctory. His, though, was properly capitalized, sincere and almost a page long. She had found herself printing it out to read it on the subway home.

They started emailing each other every day, then talking on the phone. When she went out to the Bay Area on business, they had dinner. The talk had turned to travel and the places they'd never been to that they wanted to before they died. Before she knew it, they were planning a trip to Australia together.

Before they could go to the beach, they had one more errand to do, book a room for one night in Kuranda. They'd had difficulty picking out places to stay. They were a little too old for the backpacking scene, but not so established or committed it seemed to make sense to stay in one of the luxury resorts. She could have afforded, it of course. Presumably, he could, as well–despite his company's failure, he seemed not to stress about any spending.

It just seemed silly to spend lavishly on accommodations when the trip's purpose was so indeterminate. Port Douglas would have been the perfect place for a honeymoon, or a power couple's vacation away from it all.

"One room," the woman at the office said in her soft Australian accent. More comprehensible than most, she must have been from Sydney or thereabouts. "For a couple."

"Two beds, though," he quickly interjected. His voice caught the woman's attention with its unusual urgency, as if a dreadful mistake were about to be made that could not be easily undone.

The woman blinked furiously and spoke quickly into the phone. "Sorry, love. Two beds."

Not wanting to, but she looked up at and saw the woman, still holding the phone, looking at her curiously. She shrugged and stepped to her right, to the long rows of pink, green and blue brochures on the wall. She reached for one with a catamaran sailboat on it, its strong mast supporting sails full of wind. She loved sailing. She missed that being in Chicago. Sailing on a lake, even a Great One, just wasn't the same.

She stopped listening once he launched into a complex discussion of arrangements for a day trip to Mossman Gorge. It would be easier with a car. But he didn't want to rent one.

"It's interesting that the price is the same if you book it yourself versus doing it through of these offices," he said. "I wonder how they work that out. What the business model is."

"As long as you can get a room with two beds," she said, trying to make a joke out of their earlier moment of awkwardness.

"Right," he said. "That does present an additional complication to the pricing."

She smiled tightly and glanced again at the brochures in her hand. Cooktown intrigued her. It was farther up the coast. Much farther. You had to have a four-wheel drive vehicle to get there because of the river crossings. It was very far from anywhere else, the brochure said, a thousand miles from the nearest McDonalds.

It disturbed him not to know how the tourist economy worked. Everyone seemed friendly. And what they had booked so far at Tropical Tours had more than lived up to expectations.

Still, it was odd, though, that the flow of money was so opaque to the customer. Like the reef observed from the deck of the tour-boat, all you could see were tranquil waves, much smaller than you would expect so far from shore. You had to have faith that all that lurked below were pretty fishes and psychedelic coral formations–not sharks, sea-snakes, or the nearly invisible lethal jellyfish, the ones that prevented swimming except inside of the net.

That day they went to the beach south of the point. That was the biggest decision they faced every day, which beach to go to. They walked a few hundred yards from the entrance. The beach curved out of sight into the distance; the water empty of people. They confined themselves inside the swimming net, which seemed too small for all of the swimmers; though they didn't seem to mind, splashing, laughing, and diving into the occasional high wave. Australians always seemed so cheerful.

Once they'd put down their beach mats she asked him to put sunscreen on her back. As he rubbed in the lotion, she enjoyed the sensation of his fingers pressing into her shoulder blades. His touch was amazing, but somehow impersonal. Curious, she glanced back at him as he rubbed the suntan lotion in. His face wore a look of great concentration, but not pleasure–more like he had been given a task at work and he was determined to do his best. Why did it feel so good then, as long as she didn't think about his face, but instead just closed her eyes and imagined one of the lifeguards massaging her instead.

"Should we talk about our plans?" she asked. She had been wanting to bring it up all day, and wishing that he would do it for her. However, he seemed comfortable in their routine of breakfast, beach, and then watching the sunset during happy hour, followed by dinner and an early bed-time. He seemed to need a lot of sleep.

"Sure. We should definitely check out some of that stuff the woman in the tourist office was talking about."

"What about going up the coast?" she asked. "Didn't you want to do that?"

She wished she could explain why Cooktown and Cape Tribulation held such great allure for her, without sounding like she was dissatisfied with their vacation so far. She liked the idea of going as far as they could away from the civilization, to be on the edge of the unknown. According to the guidebook, there was nothing else on the coast all the way to the tip of the peninsula except rain forest, swamp, and crocodiles, ones so large they could swallow a human being whole.

"Yeah..." he said, unnaturally extending the word. "The bus schedule is... complicated," he continued, and closed his eyes.

"I think we could figure it out," she said. "If we left tomorrow, we could spend two nights, then come back in the inland bus."

She held out the bus schedule, a thin piece of paper half the size of a normal sheet of paper, but he seemed indifferent. He took it, glanced at it, and then tucked it into his book, a paperback with a painting of a sailing ship with square-rigged sails on the cover.

"I like sitting here, looking at the waves," was his answer. "I like being here."

When they walked back from the beach, they had an hour to kill before they felt it was appropriate to have their first beer, even on vacation. She asked if they could stop by the convenience store, since her supply of reading material was running low.

Once they were inside, he snuck a look at the rack of girlie magazines while she was obsessively picking through the huge section of women's magazines, as indistinguishable to him as the men's magazines he was looking at would be too her. But he knew better. It was the same urge—the comforting thought that the things that seemed so rare in one's life (happiness with one's body, beautiful sex-starved women, ideal relationships, young women who wanted nothing more than to anonymously couple with mates not high on the evolutionary fitness ladder) were plentiful, available, and achievable.

Really, they were the same thing, or two sides of the same coin. He understood, but she wouldn't. To her the women's magazines were worthy, constructive, whereas the copy of *Penthouse* he was leafing through she would no doubt find disgusting. So why? He couldn't confront her with that truth. It was a gulf that couldn't be crossed. He knew he should put it away before he got caught, but he liked the woman in the pictorial. She was wanton, and she spread her legs in a way that seemed something more than perfunctory or obligatory, a quick payday so she could make her rent. He fixed the image of her in that pose in his mind, and then quickly slid the issue back, since he sensed she was ready to leave.

His peripheral vision was accurate. She was coming towards him, holding a stack of glossy, brightly colored magazines. He thought about crossing the gap to her, but decided that seemed too guilty, so he just waited.

Over dinner they talked about relationships, in an abstract, theoretical way, prompted by an article she had read that day in the Australian edition of *Cosmopolitan*. They got on the subject of devotion.

"What woman wouldn't want a man who adored her and would do anything for her?" she asked.

"I wonder if it's a good idea to want anything that badly," he replied.

She felt stung. She reminded herself that he had tried, tried very hard, and failed. He had mentioned, in his emails, the two years of little sleep and seven-day workweeks. Failed, but through no fault of his own? She didn't know. Nothing he had said gave any clue.

He had tried to explain what his company had done, or tried to do. She couldn't quite follow it. Something about auctions to raise money for other start-ups. To her, it sounded too removed from reality to be successful. He seemed to believe in it still, though–at least, he made long, logical arguments about why it would have been better for the world.

He seemed too detached for someone who was supposed to have been leading a company. But then his personality on this trip might be very different than who he had been at his company.

Was he just depressed due to his failure? Was that why he thought wanting was wrong? But how could anyone really live that way?

She was watching *Sex In the City*. She had turned it on while he was in the bathroom, brushing his teeth. She liked the show; and she thought maybe it would break through his strange indifference to her; his tender regard for her that also felt impersonal, as if he were a priest or a teacher of very young children.

The show was about sex, right? She giggled as one of the characters discussed the difficulties in performing oral sex. She checked to see what his reaction was. He was peering at the screen, cheeks wrinkled, looking baffled.

"Do you not like it?" she asked. "We can watch something else. She reached for the remote control.

"No, it's okay. I'll just sleep." Which is what he did. She held the remote, wanting to change the channel, but not wanting him to know that she did. She put it down on the covers, and resolved to watch it, but not giggle.

After five minutes, she looked back. He was asleep. She bit her lower lip as the characters on the screen continued to babble about difficulties it didn't seem she was going to face on the trip. It was not hard to not laugh. Or cry.

Late in the night, he woke. He listened to her slow, steady breathing. She seemed like a lonely person, which surprised him. She had been one of the most important members of their group of friends in college. She had made some sacrifices for her career, he supposed. As had he. At least she still had a job, and an industry, to go back to.

He remembered the *Penthouse* girl. He really just wanted relief. He knew he should need, and want, more than that, but it just wasn't in him.

The next morning they had their standard breakfast at the café across the street from their motel. Brekkie, the Australians called it, who never seemed to miss an opportunity to give things casual, informal nicknames. A strange nation, the way they combined baby talk and macho posturing.

He surprised her by suggesting they try a new beach, to the north of town. A bit of a walk, but worth it to get away from the crowds. It was a Saturday, and many locals had come up from Cairns. They wouldn't be able to swim, though. It wasn't a beach park, so there would be no netting, no lifeguard trained in first aid.

He pointed to the sign that described what to do if you got stung by a jellyfish. A plastic jug of vinegar hung next to it. He said that if you were desperate and had anything else, you were supposed to urinate on the person.

The guidebook had a whole chapter on the dangers of Australian wildlife. Australia seemed to have more animals that could kill you then the rest of the world combined. Most were easy to avoid. The box jellyfish, though, lurked in the water off of every beach in tropical North Queensland during the summer months, their breeding season. They had decided to come in May, without knowing that beaches would still be closed.

Their guidebook spent a lot of time describing what it was like being stung—the agonizing pain, and that's if you were lucky enough to only be get the tentacles brushing your legs or arms. If they touched your chest or mid-section, death from cardiovascular collapse could occur in just a few minutes.

A family were near them, a husband and wife, three kids. The two older ones were happy to stay out of the water and build sandcastles. Their youngest, a girl in pigtails, though, seemed to want to go in the water. She pulled on her father's arm, but he told her they had to stay on the beach.

A few minutes later, the little girl, young enough she didn't have to wear a bikini top, ran without warning towards the water. She got a few feet into the waves before the father managed to scoop her up.

The father admonished his little girl, pointing to the small waves, telling her about the jellyfish. His words were firm but kind. They didn't mean to hurt her, it was just the way they were–like bees or spiders, the jellyfish were just protecting themselves. The little girl didn't seem like she could really believe the menace was real, but she looked up at her father with trusting, adoring eyes and nodded yes.

She felt a hole welling up inside of her. She longed to feel what she saw in front of her. She felt cheated. How could she feel this alone at this stage in her life?

Her eyes burned. She wiped them with the back of her hand. She checked to see if he noticed. He was looking at her with the same ambivalent indifference with which he'd greeted the prospect of going to Cape Tribulation.

He saw her tears. A million miles from anywhere, but he couldn't escape them, either the sadness, or the indifference to the sadness that was somehow worse.

He stood and walked towards the water. He saw the filaments, glistening just below the slowly lapping wavelets–no crest, just a thin strand of foam at the top. The reef prevented the waves from becoming too large, but it couldn't keep them safe.

He entered the water. He wanted to feel something. He would.

It is perhaps appropriate that I end this collection with a selection from summer 2001. In the fall of that year my world changed very much, from both internal and external forces. My dotcom finally called it quits on August 1st, and several months later, so did my mental health.

I had followed my dreams, and it didn't work out. The experiences I had during dotcom informed Celebrated Summer, *the parallels I saw between 1989 and 1999 (only ten years apart, but it feels like far more than the years since then) and in early 2002, I began serious work on that novel again. So, this story does not represent the end of my career, but it is perhaps the end of the beginning, or the early middle. Or whatever.*